PEPPER'S RULES
for Secret Sleuthing

PEPPER'S RULES
for Secret Sleuthing

Briana McDonald

Simon & Schuster Books for Young Readers
NEW YORK LONDON TORONTO SYDNEY NEW DELHI

SIMON & SCHUSTER BOOKS FOR YOUNG READERS
An imprint of Simon & Schuster Children's Publishing Division
1230 Avenue of the Americas, New York, New York 10020
This book is a work of fiction. Any references to historical events, real people, or real places are used fictitiously. Other names, characters, places, and events are products of the author's imagination, and any resemblance to actual events or places or persons, living or dead, is entirely coincidental.
SIMON & SCHUSTER BOOKS FOR YOUNG READERS
is a trademark of Simon & Schuster, Inc.
For information about special discounts for bulk purchases,
please contact Simon & Schuster Special Sales at 1-866-506-1949 or
business@simonandschuster.com.
The Simon & Schuster Speakers Bureau can bring authors to your live event.
For more information or to book an event, contact the Simon & Schuster Speakers
Bureau at 1-866-248-3049 or visit our website at www.simonspeakers.com.
Jacket design by Krista Vossen
Interior design by Hilary Zarycky
The text for this book was set in Adobe Garamond Pro.
Manufactured in the United States of America
0820 FFG
First Edition
2 4 6 8 10 9 7 5 3 1
Library of Congress Cataloging-in-Publication Data
Names: McDonald, Briana, author.
Title: Pepper's rules for secret sleuthing / Briana McDonald.
Description: First edition. | New York : Simon & Schuster Books for Young Readers,
[2020] | Audience: Ages 8-12. | Audience: Grades 7-9. | Summary: Amateur detective
Pepper Blouse, a rising seventh-grader, cannot resist investigating when her Great Aunt
Florence passes away under mysterious circumstances, but strictly following her mother's
Detective Rulebook may not be the best plan.
Identifiers: LCCN 2020022019 (print) | LCCN 2020022020 (ebook)
ISBN 9781534453432 (hardcover) | ISBN 9781534453449 (trade paperback)
ISBN 9781534453456 (ebook)
Subjects: CYAC: Mystery and detective stories. | Fathers and daughters—Fiction. |
Single-parent families—Fiction. | Death—Fiction. | Great aunts—Fiction.
Classification: LCC PZ7.1.M434353 Pep 2020 (print) | LCC PZ7.1.M434353 (ebook)
| DDC [Fic]—dc23
LC record available at https://lccn.loc.gov/2020022019
LC ebook record available at https://lccn.loc.gov/2020022020

To Mom and Dad,
whose limitless faith made this book possible

PEPPER'S RULES
for Secret Sleuthing

RULE ONE

Your loyalty is to the case. Those who are loyal to you will come around.

Dad and I stand in front of the biggest house I've seen in my life. It looks like a row of two-story houses were smooshed together, then decorated with thick Greek pillars and pearl-white shutters. The driveway alone is so large, we had to drive around an enormous patch of frog-green grass that circles a glowing fountain with a perpetually spitting dolphin in its center just to park by the front door.

I crane my neck to take it all in, eyes wide. "It looks like a giant, haunted mansion. *Perfect* for some summertime sleuthing."

Dad gives one of my curls a playful tug. He smiles, tired but warm, and pinches my cheek between his thumb and forefinger. "Pepper, please. We talked about this."

I glance up at the mansion, enormous and brimming with potential. Dad's still waiting for the doctor to determine the cause of Great-Aunt Florence's sudden death, and my sleuth senses haven't stopped tingling since Aunt Wendy—Dad's recently divorced, semi-estranged sister—called with the news.

Especially after Dad gave me a lecture on the way over about how money adds pressure on people, even families. It seemed like a strange thing to mention—as though some subconscious part of him felt wary of the situation, even if he wrote it off as stress over attorneys and the will.

Now, seeing the bags under Dad's eyes, I deflate. My arms uncross and I let him grasp my hand in his large one. His wedding ring is cool against my skin.

"I understand," I say. "But only because you told me to."

He grins, so wide his cheeks lift. "That's not the colloquial definition of the word *understand*, but I'll take it."

I want to ask what *colloquial* means, but answering it myself will give me the chance to do small-time sleuthing in Great-Aunt Florence's library. Houses this big *always* have a library.

I tighten the straps of my favorite polka-dot backpack over my shoulders. As Dad reaches for the doorbell, the front door swings open, as though someone had been watching us from a window.

"Look who decided to show up!" Aunt Wendy stands with one hand on the doorknob and the other on her hip, dressed in a knee-length wrap dress and wearing the kind of smile that looks like invisible strings are holding up the sides of her mouth. "I was just about to send out a search party."

"Very funny," Dad says, as though the words could somehow conjure a playful laugh (they don't). "We pulled off at a rest stop on the way here, but I didn't think we were *that* late."

Aunt Wendy raises one of her penciled-in eyebrows. "Your cold dinner says otherwise. So just ditch those suitcases here and go eat."

Studying Aunt Wendy is like watching a caricature spring to life. Her thin smile and high voice match how I envisioned her whenever she called Dad. I would eavesdrop—like any good sleuth—as she listed off what she wanted him to get her family for Christmas, or offered minutes of unsolicited advice when Dad uttered phrases as simple as "Work was tiring today."

But he always indulged her orders and rants, just as he does now. He leaves the suitcases by a giant grandfather clock (classic mansion décor), then reaches to hug his sister. I wonder if, even on those phone calls, he knew she was headed for a divorce. Maybe he decided to watch what he said around her, like he told me to in the car. Or maybe this was how his relationship with his older sister has always been, since back when they shared childhood summers here, in this mansion.

Aunt Wendy turns to me next. "And Pepper." She extends

her arms and I lean in for a hug. Instead, she pinches a handful of my curls between her fingers. "Oh my gosh, did my birthday gift not reach you?" she asks, a mortified edge to her voice. "I sent a flat iron that would've taken care of this."

I tighten my grasp on my backpack straps to resist the urge to swat her hand away. As if I'd *want* to get rid of the orange curls that bounce like a giant, frizzy halo around my head, the way Mom's did. After all, my fiery hair is the reason my parents named me Pepper.

Aunt Wendy gives my backpack the same once-over she did my hair. "Why don't you take off your bag, get comfortable? We're going to sit down for dinner."

"I like to keep it on." It's stuffed with my detective supplies, like my flashlight, binoculars, and magnifying glass.

Dad lets out a soft chuckle. "It's true. She doesn't go anywhere without it."

Footsteps approach from the next room over. I turn to see a boy my age standing in the dining room. His hair is like Aunt Wendy's: blond and so flat it looks glued to his head. He has a small, upturned nose and beady blue eyes. I immediately recognize him from a picture on our fridge.

"Come in, Andrew," Aunt Wendy says. "Meet your cousin."

I figured he was scowling in that photo because it was taken at school. I hate picture day. They always ask me to say *rooster*, and just as I get to the *oo*, they snap the photo so I look like a shocked emoji. But apparently that's just

Andrew's face, because he's wearing the same look now as he glares at me from the next room over.

"Andrew can show you to the dinner table," she says. Then, wiggling her fingers, "*After* you hand me your phones." She gives Dad a tight but familiar smile. "My no-phones-at-the-table policy still stands."

Dad digs in his pocket, rolling his eyes but obliging. "It's not like I'd get much use out of it anyway. Aunt Florence never had Wi-Fi or cable, did she? I don't know why I bothered lugging my work laptop all the way here. She was never one for technology. Kind of like you."

She shrugs her thin shoulders. "I like to live in the moment."

He slaps his cell into her hand. "Maybe if you weren't so anti-technology we wouldn't have to wait for family deaths in order to see each other."

I've seen Dad Skype old friends and former coworkers before, but we only talk to Aunt Wendy over the phone. His tone is light and playful now, but there's a tinge of hurt in his eyes. Aunt Wendy must notice, because her resting-scowl-face wavers for an instant, though she doesn't return his phone.

Dad seems used to Aunt Wendy's bossiness, but I don't want to give up our phones—especially not when Dad's waiting for an important call from the doctor. I make a rebellious show of checking my notifications (nothing but an update on today's screen-time usage) before relinquishing my phone.

It's not that I have anyone to text; my classmates from West Higgins are still a bit bitter after I solved my last case. I should have never set out to prove Sophie was gossiping about Ashley with her new best friend, Vanessa. I couldn't help but hope, though, that Ashley might choose me as Sophie's replacement. And maybe I did it to help prove the theory in my bones, about the new part of me that had begun to emerge at the end of sixth grade.

That was the part that wrote Ashley's name in the bathroom stall next to all the boys' names and hearts. The part I hadn't asked Dad about yet, but kept sort-of-not-really *meaning* to. The part that prayed for a text and, at the same time, hoped it never came. Especially when Aunt Wendy had my phone.

Dad steps through the entryway, head craned up toward the high ceilings. "Exactly as I remembered it." He adjusts his glasses on the bridge of his nose and grins at Aunt Wendy. "You used to *love* this place when we were kids. I remember you exploring every nook of this old house, daydreaming about travel and adventures."

Looking at my aunt, dress perfectly ironed and each blond hair smoothed into place, I can't imagine her ever being a traveler or adventurer. That sounds more like Mom than Aunt Wendy.

Dad's smile and tone soften as he says, "You were always talking about how you wanted to be just like Aunt Florence when we grew up." His eyes flicker with realization. "And I guess you succeeded, huh? You'll have to show me those photos from your most recent stay in Europe, like you promised on the phone."

Aunt Wendy releases an exasperated laugh. Not the look I'd expect from a world traveler when asked about her adventures. "Just like Aunt Florence? As in, marry rich to afford those adventures and travel?" She waves her empty ring finger. "I tried. Look how that turned out."

Dad bites his lower lip as though he could swallow down his misspoken words.

"You go enjoy dinner," she says, our phones stacked in her free hand. "I have to finish setting up the guest beds for you."

Andrew's scowl falters and his eyes widen. "You're not eating with us, Mom?"

He shoots a sideways glance my way, as though silently telling her, *Don't leave me alone with these people.* I'd be more offended if I didn't find it so strange. Why would Aunt Wendy make a big deal about our phone-free family dinner if she didn't plan on joining it? Shouldn't she have set up the guest beds before we arrived?

Dad hesitates in the dining room entryway. "Wen, you don't have to—"

"I want to," she insists, already at the bottom of the

stairway. "Now go eat, before the food gets any colder."

I stand in the hall, watching as Aunt Wendy heads up the carpeted stairs. Dad gives the room one last wistful glance before taking my arm and guiding me after Andrew into the dining room.

I practically inhale my plate of cold chicken and green beans, eager to get my phone back. I'm pretty used to speed-eating after sitting alone in the cafeteria the last two weeks of the school year. There were days I could barely eat, hearing Ashley and the other girls laughing a few tables over and feeling curious stares burning into my lonely back. But I kept Mom's *Detective Rulebook*—her handwritten list of tips for great detective work—placed beside my lunch tray and pretended she was there, encouraging me to go after the truth at all costs.

After all, rule number one reads: *Your loyalty is to the case. Those who are loyal to you will come around.*

Aunt Wendy reenters, this time through another door leading into what looks like the library I *knew* the mansion had. Once my plate is empty, I plop my fork down with a proud *clang*. "Can I have my phone back now?"

She passes my phone over the floral tablecloth and I snatch it eagerly. "I can't promise you'll have service out here, though. It's spotty at best."

When I turn my phone on, I have a shocking zero bars. I was sure I had at least some service when I gave her my phone.

Aunt Wendy sits beside Andrew and pats his smooth, blond hair. "Andrew's only a grade ahead of you, so I'm sure you'll have plenty to bond over this summer."

Andrew scoffs. Actually, audibly *scoffs*.

Dad yawns. "I'm pretty wiped from the drive. Do you mind if Pepper and I turn in early?"

Aunt Wendy rolls her eyes and laughs softly. "Always in bed before eight. At least some things haven't changed since we came here as kids."

As we rise and head toward the main stairs, Andrew dashes off as if he'd been perched on the edge of his seat, ready to escape socializing from the second we sat down.

I try to imagine Dad and Aunt Wendy my age, playing together in this giant, wonderfully creepy house. The holiday cards she sent us listed return addresses from all over the globe, as far away from our apartment in Connecticut as can be. Other than a few phone calls a year, my dad didn't seem to spend much time with Aunt Wendy. It's tough to picture them spending an entire summer together with a great-aunt I never knew.

I make a mental note to ask Dad more about his sister later. If I can't explore the house's other mysteries, I might as well decode what *that* relationship must have been like.

Aunt Wendy ushers us up the main staircase to the second floor. I take my time on each step, pressing my weight down to check for squeaks that could suggest at secret, removable floorboards. But when Dad glances back and shoots me a glare, I remember my promise to him in the car. I hurry to meet them at the top of the stairs.

Aunt Wendy leads me down a narrow hall, past a series of closed doors and scenery paintings. "This is your room," she says, gesturing into a small bedroom with a wooden bed frame and quilted bedspread. "I'm sure you'll find everything you need."

While she hovers in the doorway, Dad leans down to plant a big kiss on my forehead. "I'll be right down the hall if you need me."

I wrap my arms around his neck, wishing for a second that I didn't have to sleep alone in this new place. But, closing my eyes and conjuring the memory of my mom, my courage reignites.

Dad releases me and heads back into the hall. Aunt Wendy makes a show of closing the door securely behind her, trapping me in the guest room.

I fall onto the quilt. Its prickly fabric scratches my skin, and I jolt back up to rub my arms. For a moment I take in my surroundings—the plain wooden dresser and chipped surface of the nightstand—before pulling out my phone.

Still no bars. It's almost as if Aunt Wendy tampered with my service. There's no reason she would do that, though, and a good detective wouldn't let paranoia cloud her judgment. But Dad did mention she was anti-technology. Perhaps she's so eager to reconnect with Dad that she sabotaged our phones.

I go to my gallery instead, clicking on a photo of my mom. It's a little blurry since it's a snapshot I took of a framed photo that rests on Dad's desk back at home. She's in uniform, posing with me and an award for excellence she earned after solving a string of local robberies. I'm smaller, but my hair is just as big, our two red heads taking up half the image.

None of Mom's coworkers believed her when she had a hunch that the robberies were staged by a collection of business owners, working together on their block to cash in on their individual insurance payouts. But she followed her hunch and pursued the lead anyway—despite everyone's objections—and proved she was right by solving the case and winning an award.

When Mom was getting ready for the awards ceremony— fluffing up her hair in the mirror rather than brushing it down—she told me that being the only female cop in her district meant it was harder to take risks, but also more important. She had to prove herself in ways the boys didn't have to. Her colleagues wanted her to prove herself by following *their* rules. But—running her hands over my poof of hair and beaming that big, toothy smile of hers—she told me that she needed to prove herself by taking that risk, following her lead, and showing that she could solve any mystery, no matter how big. Which, I'm guessing, is why she wrote rule fourteen: *Trust your gut.*

If Mom were here, she'd probably be able to fix my phone *and* figure out how I lost service in the first place. Then I could ask her about the other little mystery that was emerging inside me.

It's not that I didn't trust Dad. But I was scared if I told him, he'd take it too seriously. I wasn't sure enough to say I only wanted to draw hearts beside names like Ashley's. After all, I'd cried for a day when Tyler Waters stood me up at the Homecoming dance, and that heartbreak still felt real—just as real as the last weeks of school when Ashley avoided eye contact.

I was scared Dad would obsess over it, and I didn't even know what *it* was. But if Mom were here, she'd treat it like a case, weighing the possibilities and exploring the answers along with me. And if we discovered Ashley was a red herring, she would let it go and let me move on without feeling changed in her eyes.

My phone screen fades to black. Maybe I can't solve that mystery right now, but I might be able to figure out what happened to my phone. Dad told me to put my sleuthing on pause for the summer, but the *Detective Rulebook* says to dig deeper each time someone tells you to stop looking. To trust your hunch, even when everyone else says you're wrong.

So I follow my hunch, like Mom would want me to. With my backpack strapped on, I slip through the door and peer down the hallway.

Empty: check.

Next I slither down with my back to the wall and peek along the stairs. All clear, but I take this slower. I've already checked that the stairs aren't creaky, so I make it down silently, but still have to be careful not to be spotted the closer I get to the first floor. I crouch low to the steps, peering through the railing.

As I reach the bottom steps, I hear voices. I should be afraid, but I'm also excited; I need to determine Aunt Wendy's location if I intend to spy on her and find out the truth about our phones. I duck behind the grandfather clock, forehead pressed to the cool, wooden surface to keep myself (and my hair) from view as she approaches from down the hall.

". . . thought I told you to go to sleep," she's saying. "I have some work to get done, and you need your rest. Alanna will be by at nine tomorrow morning."

"I know, I know," Andrew whines. I peer around the clock and see them at the end of the hall, Aunt Wendy ushering him forward like she did Dad and me. Like she's in a rush to get somewhere. "I don't get why I need tutoring this summer. My grades are as good as they were last year."

"Wolestone Prep demands *better* than good," she says. "And for excellent grades, you need excellent rest."

Wolestone Prep. I hadn't heard of it, but it sounded expensive. I thought back to what Dad said about money, and how it can add pressure to families.

Andrew's pouty expression doesn't change, so Aunt Wendy leans down and plants a kiss on the top of his blond mop of hair. Her voice lowers, and I can barely make it out over the creaking of old floorboards beneath their feet.

"Only the best for you, okay?" she murmurs against his hair. "I know a lot has changed, but that won't. I promise." She straightens up and gives him a nudge toward the end of the hall. "But for that, I'm going to need you to get to bed."

Andrew huffs and heads up the stairs. I duck in the shadow of the clock and pray he doesn't spot me.

Aunt Wendy lets out a sigh of relief and heads back down the hall. She's staying on the first floor, which is a huge plus for me; that means I can spy from outside a window.

I wait for the distant slam of Andrew's bedroom door before I dash through the foyer and out the front entrance. I'm greeted by the hum of crickets and the rush of the fountain's stream.

Pressing one hand against the side of the building, I follow the wall around to the back of the house. There isn't much room to hide; the grass is chopped half an inch to the dirt, and the bushes are trimmed to plump ovals. Great-Aunt Florence must have been passionate about landscaping, and it's working against me. In order to remain hidden, I have to hop from shadow to shadow, stretching my freckled legs as far as they will go.

Toward the center of the house, I spot a stream of light

escaping onto the lawn. I slow my pace, inching forward. It's a wide bay window with thick curtains drawn back just enough for me to get a look inside.

I peer over the sill to catch a quick glimpse through the open window and into the room. Aunt Wendy's in a small office by a mahogany desk, her back to me. She drums her fingers on the wooden surface—a sure sign of anxiety—and when she turns a bit to the side, I see she's on a cell phone rather than the old landline on Great-Aunt Florence's desk. Her voice is lower and more brusque than usual.

I duck back into the bush, my heartbeat thumping in my ears. Why would she have service when we didn't, unless she really *had* tampered with our cells?

"I've taken care of it, okay?" she says, voice low and tense. "I can't have this conversation right now. We'll talk about it another time."

Another tip I learned from Mom: *Always look for the omen in the omitted.* Words like *it* sound empty, but usually refer to the meat of the issue.

"I have a delivery I need to make tonight," Aunt Wendy says, dismissive. "Meet me tomorrow. *Alone.*"

After a beat of silence I poke my head back up to the sill. I watch Aunt Wendy shove the phone into her purse before popping open the lid to a small, white box. Her body blocks its contents from view as she reaches inside. Her arm shifts, placing the lid back down. Her free hand clutches a knife covered in bloodred splotches.

I clasp a hand over my mouth to keep from gasping. I was expecting something, but not *this*.

This. Another placeholder for an omitted word. What is *this*? As Aunt Wendy grabs a wad of tissues from a box on the desk and wipes red stains from the blade, it all becomes clear. The lack of service, the expensive prep school, the *it* she mentioned on the phone . . .

On our way to the mansion, Dad had told me to put my sleuthing on pause. He'd said there was enough tension in the family since Great-Aunt Florence's death, and spying on my relatives would only make it worse.

Dad was right when he said money can tear families apart. And Aunt Wendy had torn our family apart herself and had the murder weapon right in her hands.

RULE TWO

Never be afraid to ask the right question, or you'll end up with a lot of smaller ones later on.

A unt Wendy tosses the knife into a desk drawer and leaves the office. I hurry back around the side of the house, skipping over twigs, and hide behind the bush by the front door.

I force myself to ignore a giant spider dangling from the water pipes as I watch Aunt Wendy rush down the front steps and out into the night. She holds the square box from her office gingerly in her hands. I expect her to head toward her car—parked in front of Dad's by the porch—but she heads straight down the driveway. I align myself with the dolphin statue, pushing back the sides of my puffy hair to hide from her view.

Once she's made it past the gate, I dash after her on the tips of my toes. I see her heading toward one of the four other houses on our little dead-end street. She crosses the smooth black pavement that circles the patch of grass in the center of the cul-de-sac. While Great-Aunt Florence's mansion looms at the end of the road, the other houses are about half the size and sit closer together, separated by small yards rather than sprawling grounds like Florence's. Aunt Wendy climbs the front steps at one of these houses and rings the doorbell, positioning herself with the box held up in front of her. The door opens and she slips inside.

I can't see from this distance. I suck in a steadying breath, tighten my backpack straps, and run full speed across the street toward the neighbor's house.

The front porch light is still on, so there's no way for me to get to the living room windows without being spotted. I head around the side of the house, kneeling in the dry grass. Rough dirt scrapes against my knees as I crawl, and a bug or two dashes over my fingers.

There's an open window on the right side of the house, which I hope stares into the living room or at least an adjacent room. I peer over the windowsill. The shade is pulled nearly all the way down, but there's an inch-wide gap that I peek through.

Squinting through the sliver of space, I see a small bedroom. There are sneakers and comic books scattered over the blue rug, and a martial arts uniform dangles from a hook on the back of the door. A collection of mismatched metal baseball bats lean against the corner wall.

I edge left to get a fuller image of the room and spot an unmade twin bed. Two legs dangle over its edge. I shift farther and lower myself so my nose presses against the wooden side of the house, attempting to get a better view. I see a boy playing with a Nintendo Switch, thumbs moving at lightning speed. My eyes move to his face.

That's when he looks up and spots me.

I immediately duck into the bushes. My stomach does somersaults and behind me I hear the snap of the shade being yanked open.

One of the basic rules of great detective work, Mom wrote, was *not getting caught*. How could I mess up something as simple as that?

A disgruntled voice calls out into the night. "Hey, you! Show yourself!"

I have three options. Run for it and risk my aunt finding out I was here, spying on her. Reveal myself to the angry martial arts student. Or live in this bush forever, befriending squirrels so they'll share their nuts with me for sustenance.

I settle on option two.

I rise on unsteady legs until I'm standing in front of the open window, looking up into the boy's piercing glare. He's a few inches taller than me with slim, lanky limbs that make him look as though he's been stretched out. His jaw is tight and his eyebrows press together with a scowl, but it's different from Andrew's haughty look. This one's more guarded, his lips pursed as though ready to argue with whatever I say next.

But what strikes me the most is his hair. It's dark brown but thick and curly like mine, though just on the top, because the sides are trimmed more closely to his scalp.

He crosses his arms. "Who are you?" he snarls. "I've never seen you before, and I know *everyone* in this tiny excuse for a town."

I cross my arms too, mirroring his power stance. "I'm Pepper."

"Pepper who?"

My heel shifts in the dirt. "My last name is on a need-to-know basis."

"Well, I need to know," he says, "since you're the girl snooping around my window in the middle of the night."

"All you need to know is that I'm the daughter of a late and great detective," I say, my voice inflated with false authority. "I'm on a supersecret mission."

He raises a thick eyebrow. "Involving my window?"

"Involving your guest." I'm revealing too much. I clear my throat and rummage through the *Detective Rulebook* in my mind. Number eighteen: *When in doubt, dish it out.* That was Mom's singsong reminder that when you feel you're under fire, it's time to turn the tables. "You *are* currently hosting a guest, are you not?"

The boy glances back over his shoulder toward the door

with the martial arts uniform. "My parents are. I'm avoiding the situation."

I keep up with the questioning. "And why is that?"

The muscles in his neck tighten. "That's on a need-to-know basis." He reaches for the shade. "Bring your investigation elsewhere. I'm going to bed."

He starts to pull it down. I need to act, fast.

"What was in the box?"

My voice is high and shrill, the words slurred together in a rush. But the boy pauses.

"What?" he asks, voice riddled with genuine confusion.

"Your guest had a box," I say. "Its contents are imperative to my investigation."

He rolls his eyes. "It was a cherry pie. To celebrate finding out that my mom's having a girl."

Cherry pie. Could that account for the red stains on the knife?

For a split second I consider that I've lost my trail. Perhaps Dad's anxiety over his aunt's to-be-determined death had rubbed off on me.

Then the *real* investigator genes kick in with the perfect follow-up questions. Who had Aunt Wendy been on the phone with? And what were they meeting about tomorrow?

If anything, I'm more confused than ever.

"I don't want to talk about the stupid baby anymore, and especially not with some weirdo who sneaks around strangers' houses at night." The boy gives me a curt wave. "*Good night.*"

He yanks the shade all the way down. I shift my weight foot to foot, pacing in place. My head swarms with ideas like an aggravated beehive.

For whatever reason, this boy wasn't interested in celebrating with his parents. Personally, I'd be thrilled to have a new sibling (not that *that* was ever going to happen). But he was avoiding thinking about it entirely.

Maybe I could use that to my advantage.

I knock on the glass. "I have a proposition."

I hear a long groan. "Go away!"

"You can either stay inside all summer, listening to baby talk and playing your video games—"

"How long have you been watching me?"

"—or you can solve a murder mystery with me," I say. "I could use the help of someone who knows the neighborhood."

It's silent on the other side of the window. I remain still, staring at the closed shade hopefully.

But it doesn't budge. I'm going to be alone on this one.

Just as I start to turn away, the shade snaps back open. I can't help but beam as the boy stands at the window, eyebrows raised.

"Nothing ever happens in this town," he says. "No *way* was someone murdered."

His interest is piqued.

"Our job is to prove someone was," I say, all official-like. "We start tomorrow. I'll get you when duty calls."

I want to walk off with that awesome finishing line, but there's one more thing I have to ask—even if it's not as cool of a send-off.

"What's your name, anyway?"

He bites his lower lip, as though debating if he really wants to get involved. Shrill laughter carries in from the next room, probably his mom's and my aunt's. He sighs and says, "I'm Jacob Buckley. Now let me go to sleep."

With that, he yanks the shade down with finality. This time I turn and leave, sneaking off into the night, the buzz of success coursing through my veins.

Until I regain service, I won't know if Ashley or the other girls will forgive me. But perhaps I can live with that, so long as I have a new partner by my side.

Besides, space from Ashley might give me time to figure out that other mystery. The one I had to crack all on my own.

Wherever Mom is, I hope she's watching—because this summer, I'm going to make her proud.

RULE THREE

When your first lead fails, assume there are ten more you're overlooking.

The next morning, I beat Dad to breakfast by a full half hour. I'm almost done scarfing down a banana when he finally shuffles in. He lifts his glasses, rubbing his eyes underneath. I leap out of my chair by the kitchen island and skip over to the fancy coffee maker. I hit the latte button and hold a mug underneath for him.

"You're up early," he says with a yawn, taking my open seat.

"I'm meeting a friend today," I announce proudly. Since my last case at West Higgins, I haven't had the chance to say that. The words taste sweet on my tongue.

Dad eyes me curiously as I pass the latte to him. The steam fogs his glasses. "A friend? Around here? Already?"

I puff my chest out. "That's right!"

His concerned eyes return to view as the fog clears

from his lenses. "When did you have time to meet some-one from around here?"

Oops. I backtrack, fast. "I went on a walk this morning. Aunt Florence's grounds are the prettiest I've ever seen!" Only half a lie, so I don't feel *too* bad saying it.

Dad nods, too sleepy to find holes in my explanation. "Who's your new friend?"

I toss my banana peel into the compost bag. "Jacob Buckley."

Dad's eyebrows narrow. "Buckley? As in the family across the street?"

Why did he find that strange? Had I said something to give myself away? "Yeah, why?"

He shrugs and raises the mug to his lips. "I could have sworn they had a daughter."

"They're *going* to have a daughter," I say. "But the kid my age is a boy."

The skin between his eyebrows pinches with deep thought as he traces back his memories. Then he turns to his latte instead. "It's almost the same as when we were kids," he says, peering over the rim of his cup to take in the room. "That fancy coffee machine used to be a French press your great-aunt and uncle bought from a coffee shop in Cambodia. They drank Cambodian beans exclusively after that trip—with condensed milk rather than creamer."

He sighs and the steam from his latte looks like a heavy

breath leaving his lips. "Your great-aunt cleared out the house right after your great-uncle died. She had us help her sell all the souvenirs from their travels the week of his funeral."

I pick at the edge of the counter, fingers stretched toward where the French press once sat. My chest clenches to think of Great-Aunt Florence erasing her husband from the house. I would have *loved* to have a house full of relics from adventures with Mom, if I'd been old enough to go on them when she was alive.

I'm grateful Dad can share these memories of my great-aunt, so at least I can help preserve them. "When was that?" I ask.

"You were very little," he says. "It was the last time I saw your great-aunt before . . ." His voice trails off. "I wish I had seen her more often. But it gets so busy, trying to keep up with everything at home, with just me and you."

The word *just* stings like a slap. A few years ago, Dad had mentioned wanting to meet people. As though he could *just* replace Mom, like Great-Aunt Florence did with the French press. I didn't come out of my room for days after that. It wasn't until Dad told me I was finally old enough to inherit Mom's *Detective Rulebook* that I managed to dig myself out from beneath my tear-stained sheets.

I've been carrying it with me ever since. So long as Mom's there, nestled against the ridge of my spine, I know no one can take her away. And the moment Dad gave me the book, it felt like a promise to keep her alive.

Even if it meant staying *just* us.

Dad straightens up. "Before you go, there's something I should tell you. So you don't hear it from anyone else."

The banana does a backflip in my stomach. Does Dad suspect something is suspicious about Great-Aunt Florence's death too?

"Aunt Wendy heard from the doctor last night. Your great-aunt died of a heart attack."

The blood drains from my cheeks.

A sad smile crosses Dad's lips. "I was worried she had a health condition I didn't know about. I wouldn't have forgiven myself for failing to visit for so many years. I'm glad she went peacefully."

Dad seems satisfied with this answer, but I still feel uneasy.

"I thought no one had service out here?" I say. "How did Aunt Wendy get the call?"

Dad's voice is muffled by his mug. "The landline, I suppose."

I only saw Aunt Wendy on one call last night, and it didn't sound like she was talking to a doctor. And it definitely wasn't from a landline. I went to bed before she came back from the Buckleys', so maybe she *had* taken another call. But right now, it doesn't feel like the trail ends there.

Especially after the comments Dad made about Aunt Wendy wanting Great-Aunt Florence's lifestyle since she was young. And Aunt Wendy openly admitting that her attempt at it fell through.

After all, detective rule number three says: *When your first lead fails, assume there's ten more you're overlooking.*

The doorbell rings and I jump. I snatch my backpack off the end of the island and secure it over my shoulders.

"Thanks for the coffee, hon," Dad says as I skip toward the hall. "And have fun with . . . Jacob."

I hurry down the hall, hoping to avoid Aunt Wendy on the way out. Andrew stands at the front door, stepping aside so a woman can enter.

The first thing I notice is that she's wearing a backpack, just like me, even though hers is black and doesn't have polka dots. She gives Andrew a smile so big it raises her dark, full cheeks up to her eyes. She's a bit younger than my dad and aunt and has black hair even bigger and curlier than mine.

"Mom, the tutor's here!" Andrew drawls out, a bored look on his face.

The woman smiles. "I told you, just call me Alanna."

Andrew ignores her, waiting for his mom. Aunt Wendy could come down any second now.

I rush past Alanna. I'm almost by when her eyes light up and she says, "You must be Wendy's niece! Are you joining Andrew's session today?"

Andrew looks about ready to hurl at the suggestion. I shake my head. "Meeting a friend," I say, voice rushed.

She doesn't seem to catch on. Instead she cranes her neck up toward the high ceilings, body still blocking my exit. "It's too bad you're visiting under such unfortunate circumstances. I've lived in this area my whole life, and there's no property more incredible than your great-aunt's."

I stop my shimmy to the door. Is Andrew's tutor just being nice, or is she a little *too* interested in Great-Aunt Florence's mansion?

"I've lived all over Europe," Andrew interjects. "This is *nothing* compared to some of the places I've stayed."

His tone is cutting, but Alanna doesn't seem to notice. Her attention remains on the ornate crown molding. "I think our neighborhood has its worthwhile charms."

The ceiling creaks from footsteps overhead. I need to get out before Aunt Wendy arrives.

"Nice talking, bye!" I shout as I squeeze past Alanna through the doorway. She lets out a gasp, followed by a soft chuckle. I don't look back as I sprint down the driveway toward Jacob's house.

I strut right to his window and knock on it as if it were the front door. Bouncing on the heels of my shoes, I wait for him to pull up the shade. It doesn't budge. I give the glass a good pound. There's a low groan from inside, followed by the approaching patter of footsteps.

The shade flies up. Jacob stands, wearing a gray T-shirt and glaring down at me with bloodshot eyes.

"It's *nine a.m.*," he says.

I grin. "I know. Duty calls."

"No, *you* call. And you woke me up."

"But since you're up now . . . how about responding to duty?"

He presses his palm against his forehead. "Why did I let you talk me into this?"

"You're bored and sick of baby talk."

"Rhetorical question, know-it-all." He gestures his thumb back toward the yard. "Come in the front door like a normal person, at least."

I want to object, but other than a late-night pie rendezvous with my aunt, there's no reason to suspect his parents.

"And be careful, will you? We have a rosebush." His tone is sharp, but there's a gentle flicker of worry in his eyes. I grin to myself, thinking I made a good choice to pick Jacob as an ally.

I scurry around to the front of the house. By the time I reach the Buckleys' door, it's already open with Jacob waiting for me, wearing the T-shirt he slept in and a pair of jeans.

I step into a small living room with worn-in leather couches and fraying rugs. Everything is quaint and simple, from the loose jackets tossed over the backs of chairs to half-empty mugs of coffee left on the end table. It feels a lot more like home than Great-Aunt Florence's giant house.

To me, at least. Perhaps Aunt Wendy feels more comfortable in a place like Great-Aunt Florence's: the largest, fanciest home in the cul-de-sac.

Jacob slams the door shut behind us. "Before you ask, my parents aren't home."

He moves past the flat-screen TV and leather couch and sits down at a small, circular table by the kitchen door. It has a saltshaker and piles of mismatched fast-food napkins in the center, and I realize his living room and dining room are combined.

He kicks out the chair next to him and pats its wooden seat. "So, what's this all about, Nancy Drew?"

I plop down into the chair with my backpack on. "I have reason to suspect that my great-aunt Florence was *murdered* for an inheritance."

Jacob's eyes bug out. "That rich old lady from across the street?"

"I'm her great-niece," I whisper.

Jacob rubs his chin and nods. "My parents grew up with that woman who was over last night. My mom said they were inseparable over the summers."

I can't help but wonder about this side of Aunt Wendy I've yet to see. I struggle to connect the woman who Jacob's parents have called a friend for decades with my creepy aunt. I really need to follow up with my dad on that later.

Even if it doesn't align with my hunch, I need to know the full story in order to solve the case.

"I can't *stand* her son, though," Jacob says. "He mentioned some annoying cousin of his would be joining them. I guess that's you."

I grit my teeth. "He complained about me? Before he even *met* me?" I slump back in my seat. "He's the worst."

For the first time, Jacob really smiles, his entire face lighting up.

He seems eager to vent, so I say, "We need to focus, though. This is a murder investigation."

"Why do you think that old lady was murdered?"

I tell him about how our cell service was cut off, the strange phone conversation with whoever Aunt Wendy is meeting with today, and the suspicious way we learned the cause of death.

I shimmy off my backpack and plant it in my lap. Digging through its many contents, I pull out a pair of binoculars.

"We have a perfect view of my aunt Florence's gates from your living room," I say. "We'll be able to see when Aunt Wendy's guest arrives."

Thankfully, Jacob has blinds. Perfect for detective work. I half close them so nothing but the lenses of my binoculars poke through. I hold them up to my eyes and aim toward Great-Aunt Florence's gate. It's wide open as always. I can see straight toward the spitting dolphin.

"This could take forever," Jacob says with a huff. Then, with a smirk edging across his lips, he asks, "Do you want some of the pie while we wait? I promise it's made with *cherries*, not the blood of Wendy's murder victims."

"I can hear your doubt," I snap, turning to glare at him. "Do you think I'm making this up?"

"I hope not. It'd be really messed up to invent a fake murder just to pass the time."

My heart skips a beat as a van pulls through the front gates. I'm about to call for Jacob to look when I realize its side is labeled *Peterson's Landscaping*. I watch as it parks beside Alanna's car and a man jumps out and rushes toward the front of the house, tools in hand. "I'm a real sleuth, you know. It's in my DNA."

He scoffs.

"Don't scoff," I snap. "Andrew scoffs, and we agreed, Andrew is the worst."

His eyes flash up to mine. I hit a nerve. Rule sixteen: *Always know everyone's weakness, whether friend or foe.* There was definitely something more to Jacob, what with all the baby anxiety, but his hatred of Andrew was what I had for now.

Jacob doesn't retort. Instead, he points to the window. "Isn't that your aunt Wendy?"

I peer through the binoculars. Sure enough, Aunt Wendy is making her way across the front porch, headed to where the landscaper is snipping away at an already perfectly groomed bush.

I remember crawling around the edge of the house last night, how thin the shrubbery was and how the grass was mowed down to the dirt. "We almost missed their meeting!"

"Thank goodness for me," Jacob says with a haughty laugh.

"No time for bragging in the detective world," I say. "Work now, get awards later."

I dash to the table and grab my backpack. Jacob yanks a jacket off the living room couch. "There's awards for this?"

"My mom got one when she was a police officer," I say. "She used to solve big cases. That's where I get my intuition from."

Jacob leads me out the front door. "If she's so great, why isn't she still a cop?"

I almost trip down his front steps. My throat feels tight as I say, "She died more than five years ago."

Jacob freezes and I nearly walk into him. "Crap. I'm sorry. I didn't know."

I grip onto my backpack straps and keep my eyes on my neon pink shoelaces. "It's okay. I don't really remember her, anyway."

It comes out sounding more guilty than reassuring.

Jacob falls into pace beside me. From the corner of my eye, I see he's staring at his feet too. "You can't forget her detective skills, though, since you have them in you."

I can't tell if he actually believes that, but I'm grateful for the support. Already, the piano's worth of weight on my chest is lifting. "Thanks."

He offers an awkward shrug in response.

As we head toward Great-Aunt Florence's gates, I get the tingly sense that I'm being watched. At the house beside Jacob's, an old woman stares at us from her doorstep. She's small and hunched, as though shrunken by age, and has gray hair so thin it barely covers her scalp. She's wearing a knee-length nightgown decorated with cartoonish owls.

Our eyes meet, but she doesn't break her bug-eyed gaze. I shudder. "Jacob, who's that?"

Spotting her, he scowls. "Ugh. That's Mrs. Watkins. Ignore her. Nothing good comes from being around her."

"What do you mean?"

"One time, when I was helping my mom carry the groceries in from the car, she walked right through our front door and sat in the living room like she was home," he says. "Another time, she mistook my dad for her dead husband and tried to kiss him square on the mouth. My parents tell me to be nice because she's got some old person's disease that's eating away at her mind. But she freaks me out."

He crosses the street, paying no mind as Mrs. Watkins continues to shamelessly gawk at us from her doorstep. I follow suit, casting one last curious glance her way as we take off.

We stand to the left of the gate, by the tall metal fence, covered in thick vines that block a view of the house from the road. With our noses pressed against the plump leaves, we can see between the gaps. It's like watching the scene through the holes of a honeycomb, even with the help of the binoculars. While I can make out the way Aunt Wendy holds her arms around herself, shuffling from foot to foot and averting her gaze from the landscaper's, I can't read her lips.

I frown. "We need to get closer if we want to hear."

"Closer as in the back seat of his van?" Jacob sighs. "What are you expecting to hear, anyway? That she snuck up on Aunt Florence wearing a clown mask to trigger a heart attack?"

I glare at him, but he doesn't seem to notice, eyes fixed on Aunt Wendy and hands adjusting the vines to enhance his view. "If you think I'm making this up, why are you so interested?"

His jaw tightens and he forces a shrug. "Like I said. I'm bored."

"Bored? I'd be excited if I were going to have a sister."

I'd imagined what it would be like to have a sibling a couple of times. But I made sure to never let Dad see how I felt. Especially after he tried to broach the "I might want to start seeing other people" conversation. I won't need other people if I work hard enough to remember Mom, and neither will Dad. That's what I tell myself, at least.

Through the binoculars, I see Aunt Wendy hand the landscaper a check. She could be paying him for completing some shifty task. Or—I admit with a disappointed sigh—for simply trimming the bush.

Jacob's voice rises as he snaps, "I'm not excited, okay?"

I press a finger to my lips, then point through the fence to remind him we're in hiding.

He inhales a calming breath and lowers his voice as he says, "Let's just focus on your aunt."

As he says it, the sound of an approaching car rumbles from Great-Aunt Florence's driveway. My muscles go rigid as I realize that in an attempt to hide from Aunt Wendy, our backs were totally exposed to anyone approaching or, in this case, passing by as they leave the mansion.

We flatten ourselves against the fence as the van exits through the front gate in slow motion. It circles the patch of grass in the center of the cul-de-sac, driving directly in front of us. It stops a few feet away, and even though the windows are almost fully black, I sense eyes digging into me.

I'm breathless, like a snake is coiled around my air pipes.

"We've been compromised," I whisper.

Jacob grits his teeth. "No kidding."

He releases the vines and they snap back into place. I'm motionless, weighted into the dirt, but Jacob leaps to his feet and gives my elbow a tug to take me with him. My legs are like Play-Doh as I sprint toward his front door, all the while feeling as though two giant eyes are boring into my back.

Jacob yanks me inside. He leads us to the window and

we hunch down, backs against the wall and heads pressed to the windowsill, chests heaving with unsteady breaths.

"He saw us," I say.

"I know."

"She gave him a check," I say. "It could have been for the two seconds he spent trimming that bush, but I have a hunch it's for something else."

I remember how Aunt Wendy shifted unsteadily on her feet. It was almost as if *she* were afraid. The thought makes my head spin.

"Who did the other car out front belong to?" Jacob asks. "Did Wendy have another guest?"

My eyes light up. "Andrew has his tutor over." I had completely overlooked the other stranger in the house. Perhaps the meeting Aunt Wendy mentioned on her call had nothing to do with paying the landscaper?

Jacob swats my arm fast, gaze still fixed out the window. "Look."

The van remains parked outside Great-Aunt Florence's gates. There's no exhaust trail out the back. The car is off, settled in for who knows how long. My detective instincts tell me the man is still in the car, and that this is a stakeout.

"It's an intimidation tactic," I say. "They know I know that they know I know. So they're turning on the heat."

"I only understood half of what you said, but I agree." Jacob runs a hand over his face. "Crap. They saw me, too, and they're practically parked outside my place. What have I gotten myself into?"

He slumps back against the wall, knees drawn in against his chest. I shoot one last glare at the landscaper's van before sinking down beside him.

Jacob tugs at his shoelace, head hanging. Even for the short amount of time I've had an ally, I already can't imagine working alone. Back at West Higgins, no one wanted to get involved with my cases. Now I can see why, and can't help but feel guilty.

Even though I don't want to, I say, "It's not too late for you to back out. This isn't your family's scandal."

"I'd rather deal with your family's issues than mine." His shoelace comes undone in his fingers. He still doesn't look up as he says, "I know I should be excited about having a little sister, but I'm not. I'm scared she'll be, like . . . a replacement. The daughter my parents wanted all along."

Usually I can find a clue in anything, but I'm pretty stumped with this. "Why would you think that?"

Jacob wraps his arms around his shins. His chin rests on his knees. "I'm transgender."

I recognize the term from all the searches I did online in an attempt to solve the Ashley mystery budding inside me. It suddenly makes sense why Jacob dreaded having a sister. His parents must have thought he was a girl for years. He probably even had a different name before. That's why Dad was confused when I mentioned befriending the Buckleys' son.

"I never would have known," I say. "You're such a . . . boy."

Though he tries to resist it, I see his lips twitch with a budding grin. "That's 'cause I *am*, stupid." He straightens up a bit and adds, "Plus, being tall is in my genes. I'm taller than any of the girls *or* boys in my class."

I laugh. Part of me envies how self-assured he is—the confused part that popped up when I wrote Ashley's name in the stall. The part that scoured internet forums in search of an answer, but logged off without the mystery solved.

But a larger part is just happy to hear someone talk about these things with confidence. Jacob probably used to study articles and blogs too, in search of his answer.

It makes me think that maybe someday I'll be able to name that new thing inside me, too.

I want to ask a thousand questions—about when he first suspected he was transgender, what made him know for sure, how he broached the subject with his parents. Each time I meet someone, it's like solving a mini-mystery, and my detective blood pumps faster through my veins. And maybe if I can solve the Jacob mystery, I can gather evidence that I can apply to my personal case. See what fits, what doesn't, and work from there.

I'm anxious to learn more about that side of myself. But I'm also not sure it warrants a true investigation, or if it's just a misplaced hunch.

My fear of prematurely revealing my secret outweighs my need for answers. For now, at least. So I press mute on the questions populating my head and say, "I understand why you'd want a distraction."

"I just wish they were having a boy," he says, voice smaller than I'd ever heard. "That's all."

The rumble of an approaching car interrupts us. We both jump.

"Just my parents," Jacob says.

I nod, but all I can focus on is that van, still parked motionless outside Great-Aunt Florence's house. I imagine myself sprinting across the street and—just as the toes of my sneakers reach the gate—it stirs to life and full-speed squashes me like an ant.

I shudder at the thought.

Jacob kneels in front of the window, so close his breath fogs the glass. "Maybe you should hang out here for a bit. At least until he gets bored and drives off."

I almost second-guess my hearing. It's been a long time since anyone has asked me something like that. "Are you sure? Your parents won't mind?"

Jacob shrugs. "Even if they do, it's fine. It's better than going outside and getting caught by *that* guy. Besides," he says, voice lightening, "almost all my games are multi-player."

All my anxiety slips away. The van seems smaller, farther,

something that can no longer reach me. I'd forgotten, once again, that for the first time during a case, I'm not alone. And maybe—just maybe—someone else might need me, too.

I may not be ready to open up about those other things, and I may never regain the trust of my old friends at West Higgins. But at least for right now, this feels like enough.

RULE FOUR

Take note of everything, no matter how insignificant. We're smart, but not that smart.

At first, Jacob and I check the window every few minutes for signs of the landscaper. But after a while we just focus on the games. I'm terrible, but Jacob doesn't tease me (too much, at least). It's not until Mr. Buckley asks for Jacob's help in the kitchen that I notice the sun setting over the evening sky and the empty spot where the van used to be. I instruct Jacob to be ready for another early sleuthing session tomorrow and head back to my great-aunt's house.

I skip down the Buckleys' front steps, greeted by the chirping of summer crickets and a soothing, cool breeze. Just as my sneaker hits the cul-de-sac's pavement, a strained voice calls from behind me.

"Dearie?" Jacob's neighbor, Mrs. Watkins, peers through the front door. She knocks on its surface from the inside, as though inviting herself onto the street. The cartoonish owls on her nightgown stare me down with their yellow eyes. "Did you know owls and dolphins are great friends? If the species are separated for long, it will break their hearts!"

Nothing she's saying aligns with what I learned in Ms. Welch's biology class. But I can't help but pause; *breaking hearts* makes me think of Florence's cause of death.

But Jacob told me to ignore her, and right now she's the least of my problems. I head across the street, aimed for the open gates.

As I run up the front steps, I notice Andrew's tutor's car is still in the driveway. That means Aunt Wendy will probably need to speak with the tutor before coming after me. It's not much, but it should hopefully buy me a little bit of time to talk to Dad and ask him what he knows about the mansion's landscaper. And more about his relationship with Aunt Wendy, too.

I also need to jot down what I know about the case so far. One of Mom's detective rules is to take note of everything, no matter how insignificant. Without a proper trail, there's no way to tie it all together. "We're smart," she wrote, "but not *that* smart."

When I slip through the front door, I hear Dad's voice echo through the dining area. He's laughing more than I've ever heard in ages. What in this house could he find that funny?

I sneak past the dinner table toward the adjacent living room and slink along the wall, my backpack grazing the wallpaper. Through the doorway connecting the two spaces, I see Dad sitting on Great-Aunt Florence's leather sofa. Across from him is the tutor, Alanna, *also* laughing hard enough to break a rib.

For some reason, it makes me clench my teeth. I hang back, not making my presence known.

A voice makes me jump. "Great, isn't it? I haven't had to touch my textbook for the past hour."

Andrew appears on the other side of the doorframe. He leans his shoulder against it, hands in his pockets.

"I thought having you and your dad around was going to stink," he says without a trace of tact, "but this is pretty awesome. I'm glad your dad finds her interesting. She's *basic*, compared to the tutors I had when we lived overseas."

I ignore Andrew's brag, focused on eavesdropping. Alanna says something I can't hear and Dad's smile stretches to his ears. She shifts on the couch, her knees pointing toward his.

I grip the doorframe so hard, my nails chip the paint.

"Where were you all morning, anyhow?" Andrew asks.

I hold up a finger to shush him. "With my friend Jacob," I answer in a hurry.

"Jacob Buckley?" Andrew practically spits his name. "I *hate* that kid."

"It's mutual," I say, still holding a silencing finger to my lips.

Andrew doesn't take the hint. "He's practically my nemesis. We got in a *fight* a couple weeks back."

He draws the word out, low and long, like it was a swear or something. I finally turn my attention to him, just in time to see a proud flicker in his eye.

I frown. "Jacob didn't mention getting in a fight."

Sure, Jacob was a bit grumpy, but he didn't seem violent. Andrew, on the other hand, was like a windup toy that had been twisted too tight. If his story was true, I bet he started it. I know I shouldn't assume, but Mom always said to trust my gut.

"We did. In martial arts class."

"Isn't that the point?"

Andrew shrugs. "He's been going for ages and made some comment about how my form was crap. So I ignored the instructor and initiated a *real* fight."

Something about his story nags at the back of my mind. I stare at the dark red rug and wrack my memory.

That's when it hits me. "Why were you at martial arts class?"

Color rises in Andrew's cheeks. "My therapist recommended it after my parents split. But Mom didn't make me go back after *that* happened." His voice picks up a defensive speed. "I still have his number from a group text the instructor sent. I'm just waiting for the perfect prank to get revenge."

He needs me to know he can still even the score. My mind is snagged on another detail. "I meant why were you there *weeks* ago?" I press. "I thought you arrived yesterday, same as us."

If Aunt Wendy and Andrew arrived weeks ago, then they were here when Great-Aunt Florence died. That placed Aunt Wendy at the scene of the crime. She may have even known the cause of death before the doctor called, which would mean she had something to hide when she tampered with our cells.

And the fact that she was lying about when they arrived—and having her son do the same—meant she was *definitely* hiding *something*.

Andrew's eyes grow to the size of the decorative plates hanging on the wall behind him. "Forget I said that."

I crinkle my nose. "When has *that* ever worked for you?"

He bites his lower lip before sprinting into the next room. "Pepper's home!"

Dad and Alanna jump, leaping back to their respective ends of the couch. They look as guilty as Andrew, and it makes the hairs on my arms rise.

Dad adjusts his glasses and clears his throat. "Honey, when did you get here?"

Before I can answer, the clack of Aunt Wendy's shoes approaches. I sense her right behind me but can't will myself to turn.

"Alanna, you're still here?" Aunt Wendy calls over my head. "Did Andrew run into trouble with the material?"

"Not at all." Alanna springs to her feet and smooths down her pencil skirt. "In fact, I was about to head out."

As Alanna exits through the dining room's second doorway, my aunt's attention turns back to me.

"I can't get over the fact that you wear this thing inside!" She laughs, fingers drumming my backpack straps. "You should let yourself get comfortable, silly."

I swear my skin is just one giant goose bump at this point.

I cross my arms so the straps can't slip off. "I prefer to keep it on."

My dad smiles. "She's like a little turtle."

I wiggle, shrugging her off. She runs a hand against her blond hair, then steps around me.

"I'm going to freshen up before starting dinner," she announces, crossing the dining room. "Wait until you try this wonderful bread I found at the bakery yesterday. The carbs are worth it."

"Wendy," Dad calls, sitting up straight. "After dinner, can we talk about the will?"

She pauses to regard my dad. "Always so down-to-business, Frank."

She leans over him. I step forward instinctively.

But all she does is plant a kiss on his forehead. "After everything with Brandon, I'm exhausted by lawyers. A bit more time and we'll settle it all. I promise."

Aunt Wendy straightens up, smiling softly. Dad gives her hand a quick squeeze. "I know, Wen. I'm in no rush. Take whatever time you need."

Aunt Wendy turns and grins—actually *grins*—over at me. "Your dad has always been obsessed with rules and deadlines. He never would have left the guest room the summers we spent here if it weren't for me."

Dad raises his eyebrows and chuckles, as though this is a conversation he and Aunt Wendy have been having for years. "Aunt Florence made her rules pretty clear." He holds up his fingers, listing them from memory. "Don't touch her collections, stay out of the basement, and be in bed by eight."

Aunt Wendy laughs. "Thankfully, I only had one rule: that after eight, none of Aunt Florence's rules mattered."

It makes my skin itch to think of Aunt Wendy having her own rulebook of sorts. Especially when her rule let her break any that were set by others. It makes me wonder how many other rules she's broken over the years—perhaps even in the past couple of weeks, since returning to the mansion.

"Your dad knew better than to argue with his big sister," Aunt Wendy teases. Dad rolls his eyes, but doesn't look offended in the least. "If he wasn't so easy to persuade, we would have never had the adventures we did those summers."

For some reason, seeing Aunt Wendy act like a sister creeps me out as much as her acting like a murderer. Dad and Aunt Wendy shared a lot more history—and love (ew)—than I thought. It's hard to picture my tightly wound aunt as the younger, adventurous version of herself. I imagine a girl like me, but with Aunt Wendy's smooth blond hair. I imagine her tugging Dad by his wrist down Great-Aunt Florence's stairs, coercing him into a nighttime exploration of the mansion.

It doesn't align with the version of Aunt Wendy in my mind and my clues. It leaves me unsettled.

"Too bad you kids can't see this place how it used to be," Aunt Wendy says, a distant look in her eyes. "Creeping around these halls at night and digging out Aunt Florence's travel souvenirs was like going on a scavenger hunt around the world." She wraps her arms over her chest as she says, tone darkened, "But I guess selling everything after Uncle passed saves us grief now. It's easier for the lawyers to deal with the profits rather than the items themselves."

The word *profits* lingers in my mind. But I can't decipher the distant look in Aunt Wendy's eyes. Is she nostalgic for the items, and the memories they hold? Or longing for the payoff?

Aunt Wendy takes off down the hall, leaving me with Dad. I join him on the couch. "Dad, I have to tell you about my day . . ." My voice trails off as I notice his hands. Or, rather, the glaring lack of a wedding band on his ring finger.

"What?" he asks, smiling gently.

His voice is barely audible over the thumping in my head. I reach out and press my fingertip against the pale circle of skin where his ring should be. His lips part with a silent *oh*.

"Pepper, I—"

A shrill cry from the hall interrupts. "How *dare* you?"

Dad and I leap off the couch and dash down the hall. Aunt Wendy stands outside the doorway to Great-Aunt Florence's office—the one I saw her in with the knife. Her cheeks match the white of the linoleum tiles, and her chin trembles as she speaks. She clenches and unclenches her shaking hands.

"How *dare* you!" she says again, voice high and splintery. "Coming into *my* home, invading *my* privacy. Who do you think you are?"

Alanna appears at the edge of the back hallway. "I got lost on my way to the bathroom," she says, voice quivering.

Aunt Wendy inhales sharply, her nostrils flaring. "Get out. Get out *now*, before I call the police."

She is visibly shaking from head to toe. She's seemed on edge since we arrived, but right now she looks about ready to completely unravel.

Whoever Aunt Wendy was years ago—sneaking around the mansion at night with my dad—is long gone, replaced by an older, colder version. One that's trembling with a mixture of fury and fear.

What could she possibly be hiding in that office that she's *this* terrified of being found?

Dad steps forward. "I'm sure it was a misunderstanding."

Alanna shoots him a grateful smile. My intestines coil in a knot.

"You can't know that for sure," I say.

I only meant for Dad to hear it. No, actually. I meant to keep it to myself. Or at least I *wish* I had. I clasp a hand over my mouth as Aunt Wendy's trembling ceases and Alanna's shoulders slump.

I'd done what no good detective should ever do: compromise a case for personal reasons.

Dad doesn't argue as Aunt Wendy points a bony finger toward the front door; my comment—along with his desire to appease his anxious sister—has silenced him. Alanna wraps her arms around herself and hurries out wordlessly.

I should object, speak up on her behalf, but I don't. I watch her pull the door shut behind her and hope that once it closes, my dad will put his ring back on.

RULE FIVE

Know the difference between an assumption and a hunch.

I head outside for some fresh air. My gut is one big tangled mess and there's no way I can shovel down dinner while Aunt Wendy glares at me over the lazy Susan. Or while Dad holds his utensils with ten bare fingers.

Aunt Wendy said that Florence stripped the house of memories of her husband, and thinking of Dad without his ring doesn't feel much different. I realize for the first time that I don't even know my great-uncle's name or anything about him, other than that he traveled with Great-Aunt Florence. Maybe if she'd kept the things they'd gathered together, I would have heard about him. Maybe if she'd chosen to remember him, I could have too.

Dad removed his ring. He could choose to forget Mom.

A terrified voice at the back of my mind asks: *What if I told him my secret and he decided to move on from me, too?*

As I make it down the front steps, I spot Alanna's car, still parked behind Dad's. It's been almost ten minutes since Aunt Wendy kicked her out; why hasn't she left?

Yesterday I snuck around the house and secured a clear view of Great-Aunt Florence's office. Maybe Alanna *had* been snooping. Did she suspect Aunt Wendy too?

The thought gives me an excited rush that lasts half a second before my stomach drops. If Alanna's investigating Aunt Wendy, it means she has detective instincts like me.

Like Mom.

I grip my backpack straps so tight my nails pinch my palms.

I plop onto the pavement and lean against the edge of the fountain. The contents of my backpack poke against my spine, so I shrug it off for the first time in hours and dig out the *Detective Rulebook*.

That's when raised voices come from the end of the driveway, by the front gates—where I saw the suspicious landscaper. My instinct is to rush over and spy from the bushes, but the last time I did that, the landscaper caught me. A good detective knows better than to repeat the same mistake twice. I rummage through my spy equipment, searching for a solution.

My cell phone rests on top of my metal flashlight. Aunt Wendy may have messed with my service, but not all my apps require a signal. I unlock my screen and select the voice recorder. It may be easy for the landscaper to spot me through the bushes, but if I can get close enough to drop my phone into the grass, the app can do the spying for me.

The fountain is in the center of the driveway, directly in view of the open front gates. I keep far to its right and trek across the side lawn. The freshly mowed grass is like a green carpet beneath my sneakers. I move forward silently, grateful the extremely efficient landscaper prevented the swish that overgrown grass would create around my ankles.

The gate appears to grow in size as I approach. The voices become clearer and I recognize Alanna's, though it's tense and fast. I'm dying to know what she could possibly be fighting with the mysterious landscaper about, and it takes all my self-control not to pause and listen.

I place my phone in the grass, press the red record button, and retreat back toward the house. My instinct is to run, but I take my time, sure not to make a sound.

I position Mom's *Detective Rulebook* in my lap and take out a pen. Before I open the book, I run my finger over its black, textured cover. I press it against my chest and close my eyes, doing all I can to ignore the van. The book feels small in my arms, and I wonder if I've grown or if I'd always just imagined it bigger.

I flip past Mom's rules to the blank pages in the back and start to jot down everything I've learned on my case so far, starting with the most recent and biggest reveal of all.

1. Aunt Wendy and Andrew have been in Maine for weeks, which means
2. They were present the day Great-Aunt Florence died, which means
3. Aunt Wendy and Andrew are liars

Okay, that last one isn't news. But at least now I can own it as an indisputable, objective fact.

4. There's something in Great-Aunt Florence's study that Aunt Wendy is afraid of someone finding
5. A landscaper with tinted windows (who's in cahoots with Aunt Wendy? Or Alanna?) is stalking me
6. Great-Aunt Florence died of supposedly natural causes

That last fact places a giant question mark hovering over all the others. But at least I have a lead now. Tomorrow I'll sneak into the office and find whatever Aunt Wendy tried to hide from Alanna.

Someone lets out a small gasp, and I look up to see Alanna a few yards away from the fountain, paused mid-step. She presses a hand to her chest as she steadies herself. The whites of her eyes are enlarged as she looks me over.

She clears her throat. "I'll be going now," she says in an

almost apologetic tone. I silently watch as she rushes toward her car, clenching her keys in a death grip.

I remain as still as the dolphin statue as she speeds down the driveway and through the gates. When the squeal of her tires fades off, I swing my backpack over my shoulders and sprint across the lawn for my phone.

As I snatch my cell from the grass, I hear the van's engine roar to life on the other side of the vine-covered gate. Even if he couldn't see me, he may have heard me spying on him.

Gravel crunches beneath the van's tires as it rolls onto Great-Aunt Florence's property. He's already worked on the lawn and talked to both Aunt Wendy and Alanna, which means that this time, he's coming for me. And after catching me spying, he's probably not looking to just talk.

I shove my phone into my back pocket and run for the front door.

The van rumbles up the driveway behind me. My focus remains on its shiny handle like the light at the end of a tunnel.

I pump my arms and keep my eyes fixed on the doorknob. It seems farther away with each step, like I'm caught in a slow-motion nightmare, running from a flood or tornado.

A window rolls down with a mechanical whir, and a gruff voice calls out to me.

I take the front steps two at a time. The doorknob resists

as I twist, and I jiggle it with all my strength. At last it gives, and I stumble inside, slamming and locking the door shut behind me.

"Nice out there?"

I jump as Dad strolls down the hall toward me, a light grin on his face.

When he reaches me, I grab his sleeve and guide him to the dining room window. "Dad, you have to see—"

Wheels screech in the distance, fading as the van peels off. It will be out of sight by the time we pull back the shades.

The last thing I need is for Dad to think I disobeyed his no-sleuthing request, and with zero results to prove its worth.

I'm scared enough of losing him as it is.

So I drop his hand and mumble, "Never mind."

He clears his throat. "Actually, Pepper, I did want to talk."

I don't want to talk about what happened with Alanna. Or anything else rattling around in my mind. So I respond with a question. "Can you tell me about Aunt Wendy and Uncle Brandon's divorce?"

Dad blinks, startled. He gestures to the small bench in front of the dining room's bay window. I take a seat, my backpack pressed against the wall.

"What brings that up?" he asks, lowering himself onto the bench next to me.

I shrug. "Just curious. Andrew seems a bit stressed by it all."

And Aunt Wendy's comment about marrying rich, of course. How, growing up, she wanted to be just like Great-Aunt Florence, traveling the world and building high-end collections. But I can't mention that to Dad—especially after he sided with Aunt Wendy on both the lawyer and Alanna just to appease her.

He wraps an arm around my shoulder. It's warm and grounding, but a part of me resists the contact, thinking of the missing ring on his finger. "Your uncle Brandon left them so unexpectedly. I can't imagine what Andrew's going through."

I can, I think. Losing a father through divorce wasn't much different from losing my mom. For years, they're the seams holding together the fabric of your day-to-day life. Then, suddenly, they're a foggy memory—built from one photo saved on a phone, and the squiggly cursive of their handwriting.

I finally lean into Dad's arm. His empty finger feels foreign, but I'm desperate to cling to the rest of him while I can.

"It's good timing that we're able to stay here while we work out the will," Dad says. "It's been over ten years since Wendy's had a job, so it's been tough on her and Andrew financially since Brandon left. They're receiving child support, but she's fighting for more. They were used to a certain lifestyle, and Andrew was in the process of transferring to a private middle school . . ."

Motive. I know I should add it to the book, but make no move for my backpack. Aunt Wendy is listed as the primary suspect in my notes at the back of Mom's *Detective Rulebook*, but listening to my dad talk about how Uncle Brandon left her behind—how he chose to forget her and Andrew—makes me pause.

Perhaps I want to gather as many facts about my suspect as I can. But I also want to know her, the woman she was before Uncle Brandon left.

After all, I—like her—am no stranger to loss.

Dad shifts to the side, digging in his back pocket to retrieve his wallet. He fingers through credit cards and a punch card for his favorite coffee shop, then reaches a bundle of wallet-size photos. On top is an image of him and Mom, with my toddler self nestled between them on a loveseat. Dad flips it to the back of the stack, but the image imprints like a stamp in my mind. The three of us, immortalized in a photo, on Dad at all times. Nestled in his pocket, no matter what changes in the world around us.

Perhaps he won't forget us so easily.

Dad retrieves the picture he'd been searching for and holds it out for me to see. "Wendy's pretty terrible about taking photos—living in the moment and all—but she gave me some copies of their trips as a family." He smooths the top picture to reveal a photo of Aunt Wendy, Andrew, and a man I've only seen in photos, clustered together in front of the Eiffel Tower. "She says it's because she wants them gone. But I think she's hoping I'll hold on to them until she's ready to remember again, if only for her and Andrew's sake."

He tilts the photo toward me for a better look. Aunt Wendy's wearing sunglasses, so I can't see her eyes. But her smile stretches up to the corners of her cheeks—wider than any I've seen on her since arriving.

"Your aunt and Andrew spent a good portion of time abroad the past few years, traveling for Brandon's work. Wendy always dreamed about that—traveling, discovering new places, like we did together in this house as kids. We used to go through Florence's collections and pretend we visited all the countries our aunt and uncle did."

His thumb brushes over the curve of Aunt Wendy's smile. "When we were kids, she had a map she'd mark with the places we 'visited.' One year she begged Florence to visit France so she could mark it off. Aunt Florence said it was too touristy, and wouldn't go. It was up to Wendy to find a way there herself." His finger grazes past Aunt Wendy's face, up to the tower behind her. "Wendy swore she'd grow up and see the world for real. And in a way, she did. Even if it was short-lived compared to Aunt Florence's adventures."

He flips the photo to the back of the small pile, revealing

an image of Aunt Wendy and Andrew beaming, tanned and wearing sunglasses, in front of a crystal-blue ocean. It looks nothing like the murky gray sea here in New England. Their blond, smooth hair looks bright as the sun in front of the stark blue waves. "Coming back here, to where our adventures started, is probably the most normal she's felt since the split. But I bet she wishes the traveling didn't have to end for Andrew and hopes that someday they can get that part of their life back, even if Brandon won't be with them."

I tug at the edge of the first photo, slipping it from beneath Aunt Wendy and Andrew's beachside selfie. A wrinkle on the photo writes a papery white line over Uncle Brandon's face, but I can still make out the semblance of a smile. He looks happy. At home with Aunt Wendy and Andrew, even halfway across the world from their house in California.

"I've never been as much of an adventurer myself," Dad goes on. "But perhaps I was so used to letting Wendy drag me along that I gravitated right toward your mother when we met. She was never someone willing to settle, either."

I don't like to think of Aunt Wendy and Mom as similar— even after seeing this new side of Aunt Wendy in the photos. My attention remains on the picture in my hands. "How did Uncle Brandon just decide to leave like that?" I ask. "What made him wake up one morning and decide he no longer wanted his family?"

They're *people*, I think. Not furniture, or old appliances meant to be replaced.

"Sometimes," Dad says, "people change. And not always for the best."

Aunt Wendy had changed. Seeing these photos, she looked like a different woman. The kind who was eager to try new things. Not the kind who screamed at someone for taking a wrong turn on their way to the bathroom.

Dad rubs his hand up and down my arm. His fingers are warm and smooth without the gold band. Was Dad changing too? Was he leaving our family behind?

Would he leave *me* if I told him the truth about Ashley? About me?

He kisses the top of my head. Or, rather, my hair, because there's too much of it for his lips to reach my scalp.

Just like Mom's hair, that day she fluffed it up in front of the mirror. Just like Mom in one of the rare, clear memories I still have of her—and in the photo Dad keeps in his pocket like a final promise to her. To our family.

Dad opens his palm for the photo. I hesitate. "You promise to keep these? In case Wendy or Andrew ever wants them back?"

He chuckles softly. "Of course."

I place the photo in his hand, covering his ringless finger. Dad inhales sharply, as though gearing up for a speech. I quickly say, "I'm kind of tired, Dad. I think I'm going to lie down for a bit."

He nods against my hair and gives me one last squeeze. I curl into it, closing my eyes and inhaling his familiar scent, like old books and parchment.

Then I let go.

RULE SIX

All clues are created equal.

I dawdle the next morning to gather information about Aunt Wendy's schedule. A little bit of breakfast-time eavesdropping informs me that she'll be out of the house from three to four p.m. for Andrew's therapy session. It's not much time, but it's enough for Jacob and me to sneak into Great-Aunt Florence's study and find whatever Aunt Wendy is trying to hide. Or what Alanna was looking for.

I sit at the kitchen table, cell wedged in my back pocket. I haven't listened to the recorded audio yet. I'm saving the first listen for my visit to Jacob's house.

After slurping up the last of my cereal milk, I make a beeline for the door. Dad hooks his finger through my backpack loop and tugs me back.

"Slow down there, tiger," he says with a laugh. "Heading over to your new friend's place again?"

Aunt Wendy, still seated at the dining room table, gives me a pointed glance over the top of her coffee mug. I wonder if the landscaper told her that he'd caught me snooping yesterday. Twice.

Dad places his hand on my shoulder and leads me into the hall. He drops his voice to a whisper. "I wanted to tell you something before you head out."

His hand is warm on my shoulder, still with no trace of the cool wedding band.

But what he says next takes me off guard. He kneels in front of me in the entryway and says, "You're a lot better at sleuthing than I give you credit for. I've always tried to explain away your aunt's behavior because she's my sister, and because of all she's going through right now. But after that scene by the study last night, I think you might know her true nature better than I've wanted to admit."

Pride inflates like a balloon in my chest. I bite down hard on the inside of my cheek to keep from grinning like a maniac.

For a split second, I think I may have overreacted last night. But then Dad adds, "That's why I'm meeting with Alanna today. I need to apologize for how Wendy treated her."

The balloon in my chest pops. Instinctively, I shrug Dad's hand off my shoulder.

"I meant it when I said Alanna could have been snooping," I say, even though I'm still not sure if that's true. There was her strange connection to the man in the van. But this is a small town. It's possible she knew him outside of the case. But given all the other evidence, I couldn't overlook it. No matter how badly I wanted to prove Aunt Wendy was the murderer.

Rule number five: *Know the difference between an assumption and a hunch.* Right now, I'm failing that miserably.

Whether I'm right or not, I wish Dad would believe me. Or at least hear me out. I wonder if this is how Mom felt when her coworkers didn't listen to her because she was the only woman on the squad. Even Dad's willing to believe a stranger over me, just because I'm a kid.

When Mom faced pushback, she pursued her lead harder. Which means I have to do the same.

"It was an honest mistake," Dad says.

I can't hide a frown. "You don't know that. You don't know *her*."

A dark flicker of hurt crosses his eyes. "Pepper, honey, we should talk."

I wiggle past him, toward the door. "I have to go. Jacob's waiting for me."

Before he can stop me, I dash out the door, slamming it shut.

Jacob sits on his front steps, tossing a baseball up and down. He stares at a patch of dry grass with a bored look in his eye before he spots me and perks up just a bit.

"What do you know about baseball?" he asks the second I step foot on his curb.

"I know that's what you're holding."

He sighs, slumping against his front door. "My dad was supposed to practice with me today."

I join him on the front step, drawing my knees in against my chest. "I thought you did martial arts."

He rolls the ball between his palms. "I do. But baseball is my dad's favorite sport, and I figured playing it with him would give me a leg up over his unborn infant daughter."

I bump my shoulder against his. "You mean your *sister*."

He groans. "Whatever."

I crane my neck to glance through the house's front window. "Where are your parents?"

Jacob tosses the baseball. It soars a few feet before rolling across the lawn. "They ditched me to go build their baby registry. As we speak they're probably at Macy's picking out pink onesies and wishing I hadn't made them donate all of my old stuff."

I want to find the right words to cheer my friend up, but what he's going through is nothing I've ever experienced before. I have no idea what to say to make it right.

"Do you have anyone to talk to about all of this?" I ask. Mostly because I'm concerned and don't know enough to support him as much as I want. But partly because I'm unsure of who to talk to about my own secret mystery.

He shrugs. "I've been seeing a gender therapist for a few years now, since I first told my parents I felt like—since I *am* a boy. And I have a sort-of community online." He rolls the ball over in his hands. "But a lot of the people I talk to know more about transitioning as an adult. They don't have a lot of advice on being replaced by baby sisters."

I place my chin on my knees, close so it muffles my voice. "If it makes you feel any better, my dad took off his ring and was flirting with Andrew's tutor last night."

"Why would that make me feel better?"

"I don't know. Solidarity?" Jacob's expression doesn't change, so I switch to a diversion tactic. I withdraw my phone from my back pocket. "Anyway, I have a new clue. I overheard the landscaper and tutor arguing last night and was able to record the conversation. I waited so we could listen together."

Jacob tries to hide a satisfied smile. "Let's hear it."

I pull up the audio file and press play. The recording starts halfway through Alanna speaking.

"*—want you to contact me anymore.*" Her voice is wobbly, like a loose floorboard. "*This has to . . . it has to stop.*"

The landscaper's voice is gruff, but with a surprisingly soft edge. "*You can't act like this is just me. You can't possibly blame it all on me.*"

Alanna starts and stops about five sentences before she settles on, "*I want to leave this behind me. I need to leave it behind me so I can move on.*" She clears her throat, and when she speaks again, her tone is sterner. "*You should do the same, Randy.*"

The conversation trails off. The next thing I hear is Alanna's voice in the distance when she spoke to me by the fountain.

I sense Jacob grow stiff beside me. His eyes flash, glaring across the cul-de-sac, and the muscles in his neck tighten.

"Did you hear a clue?" I ask, pressing stop.

He continues to stare straight ahead as he says, "Look who showed up."

Rolling down the circle of pavement at a creepy five miles per hour is none other than the landscaping van. It slows to a halt outside Great-Aunt Florence's gates in the same exact spot as the day before. The engine cuts off, but no one comes out.

I wrap my arms around myself. "He chased me last night."

Jacob gawks. I place my hand on his forearm in the hope that he'll relax his body language.

"After Alanna left, he drove toward me as if he was going to reach out the window and snatch me right up. He may have heard me through the gate. Or"—my voice rises—"maybe Alanna told him she saw me in the yard. She passed me on the way to her car and jumped when she saw me. If they're accomplices, she might have told him I was spying, and he may have chased me as an intimidation tactic." I nod toward the van. "Like he did yesterday and like he's doing now."

Jacob rises from the steps. I grab a handful of his jeans. "What are you doing?"

He shimmies from my grip. "Playing baseball." He moves like a cartoon character in slow motion across the grass, bending over to grab the ball. When he stands up, he gives me a pointed stare. "Want to join?"

He tosses the ball between his hands again, but this time the motion is faster and backed with more force. As I glance between the van's dark windows and the ball, his plan clicks in my mind.

I position myself at the edge of the lawn, so my back is facing our stalker's car. "I have to warn you," I say at full volume, "I'm not a good catch."

Jacob smirks. "Perfect."

He beats his sneakers against the dirt, positioning himself for the throw. His arm winds back and I lift my hands up as if I intend to catch it. Then, as he pitches the ball at full force, I duck to the side and let it soar past me, straight for the van.

The baseball smashes against the driver's window and shatters the tinted glass. A voice hollers out.

"Oops," Jacob calls out. "My bad."

Startled by the sound, Jacob's old neighbor Mrs. Watkins stumbles onto her front lawn. We all stare, wide-eyed, through the shattered window. Two meaty hands block the driver's face, protecting him from the shards of glass. A fat metal ring shimmers in the sunlight.

Jacob and I step to the edge of the curb. The man lowers his hands to reach for the keys. As the engine roars to life his face is exposed in plain daylight. Square, prickly jaw. Cracked, sunburned skin. Hair buzzed so close to his head, I can see his scalp. I've branded his image in my memory by the time he peels off down the street, leaving a trail of exhaust in his wake.

When the van is out of sight, Jacob and I exchange a high five. "We did it!" I cry, literally jumping for joy.

Jacob plants his hands on his hips and puffs out his chest. "That's what he gets for underestimating us!"

I loop my thumbs through my backpack straps. "I wish your dad had seen that throw. I'm sure he would have been so proud."

Jacob's cocky smile is replaced by a sheepish one. "You think so?"

"Other than the vandalism part, yeah."

"He'll be even more proud when we solve this thing," Jacob says. "And so will your dad. I bet it will remind him how great your mom was."

I glance down at my sneakers, that unsteady feeling rising in my stomach again. "I sure hope so."

Jacob nudges my shoulder with the tips of his fingers. "Well, detective? What's next?"

"I think it's safe to say Randy is involved in *something* sketchy. Innocent people don't drive off from accidents—

especially when they're the one who got hit. It was like he was scared someone would call the police." Over Jacob's shoulder I see Mrs. Watkins squinting at us. Guilt rushes through me and I say, "But we should probably pick up all that glass."

As we cross the street I tell him about Aunt Wendy's tantrum when Alanna stepped into Great-Aunt Florence's study, the phone call Aunt Wendy claimed to get from the doctor, and how I caught her and Andrew in a lie about when they first arrived.

"That puts her at the scene of the crime," I say, kneeling on the hot pavement. A small, barely visible shard of glass pinches my knee. I shoulder off my backpack and sift through its contents until I find an empty mason jar I keep for collecting evidence. Or in this case, dangerously broken glass. "Why else would she lie about when she arrived at Aunt Florence's unless she's guilty?"

Jacob drops a handful of glass into my jar. "I figured you knew they'd been here a while. Otherwise I would have said something."

I think about my conversation with Andrew, that smug grin when he talked about quitting martial arts. "You also didn't mention getting into a fight with my cousin."

Jacob laughs. "He called it a fight? He charged me and I put him in a hold until the instructor came over."

I pinch a piece of glass between the tips of my fingers and drop it into the jar. "It seems like this divorce was a

lot worse than my dad let on. They were constantly traveling and going on adventures together abroad, as a family.
Totally different from what their life is now." Thinking of
that photo feels more like a dream than a memory. That
version of Aunt Wendy is so foreign, it's as though she never
existed. "If it's left Andrew this emotionally unstable, what
does that say about his mom?"

When I look up, I notice Mrs. Watkins waving to us
from the edge of the sidewalk. The glass slips in my fingers
and jabs my skin.

Jacob extends his hand palm-up. "You're going to break
yourself, silly."

"Your neighbor," I whisper. "She's staring again."

He rolls his eyes. "I told you. She does that."

But when she calls out, he jumps. "Excuse me, dearies?
A moment, please?"

I drop the glass into Jacob's palm. "Does she usually do
that?"

His face turns a green hue. "I've never dealt with her
without my parents!"

Mrs. Watkins waves her hands over her head so the
loose skin under her arms sways.

Eyes locked on the strange old woman, I whisper to
Jacob, "The other day, she mentioned owls and dolphins
being great friends. Any idea what that means?"

"Considering it's Mrs. Watkins, it may not mean anything," he says. When I shoot him a pointed glare, he sighs and considers the comment for a moment longer. Then his eyes light up with recognition. "She *was* close with your great-aunt, and your great-aunt had the landscaper install that ugly dolphin fountain. Maybe that was her nursery-rhyme way of telling you that?"

I nod excitedly. "Maybe she has a clue!"

Jacob catches my arm as I try to pass. His grip is steel-tight. "Or she could be dangerous. She can get . . . *confused* sometimes. Not know who you are, or where she is."

I frown and wrestle from his grip. "Just because she has a bad memory doesn't mean she's dangerous. She might know something about the case."

Ignoring his pleas, I move across the street to join her. Jacob groans, then rushes up behind me.

Mrs. Watkins leans down, dropping her voice to a whisper. Her breath smells like dead fish, but I know better than to lean back. "Come inside, dear. There's so much I need to tell you."

I nod and move to follow her. Jacob extends his arm in front of me. "Whatever you need to say, you can tell us out here."

Her eyes turn to him. They're wide and glossy and a bit red around the edges. "We can't risk them hearing."

"Who's *them*?" I ask.

She presses a hand against her chest. "I think you know, don't you, dearie?"

As she says it I swear I feel the shadow of Great-Aunt Florence's mansion hovering over us.

I place my hand softly on Jacob's arm. "She's right. We have to be discreet."

He clenches his jaw but lowers his hand to his side. Silently, we follow Mrs. Watkins inside.

RULE SEVEN

Always look for the omen in the omitted.

Mrs. Watkins's house is infested with owls. Ceramic owls on her cabinets. Knitted owls sewn into the fabric of her rugs and pillows. A mantel clock with owls carved along its sides. Glass owls holding up lampshades with their heads. Their bulging eyes ogle us from every corner of the room, and I can't help but stagger back as the sheer volume overwhelms me.

Jacob clenches his hand around my arm. "This was a mistake," he hisses under his breath.

Mrs. Watkins waddles into the adjacent dining area and settles into a rickety chair at the table, across from a full cup of tea. She kicks out the seat across from her with a slipper-clad foot. Without removing my backpack, I settle into it. Jacob grips the back of my chair and hovers over me.

Mrs. Watkins lifts the teacup to her lips with unsteady hands. She sputters and the liquid dribbles down her chin.

"Cold," she says. I resist the urge to dab a napkin to her face.

Jacob doesn't hide his impatience as he asks, "What did you want to tell us?"

Her cup clinks against her saucer as she lowers it. "Since we lost Florence, this street has been filled with liars. But I finally found a way to the truth."

I exchange a glance with Jacob. "Which is?"

If Mrs. Watkins hears me, she doesn't show it. She stirs the cold tea with a wrinkled finger. "No one else looks out for old widows like us. We only have each other."

"A group of truth-seeking widows will reveal Florence's killer?" Jacob asks, voice heavy with skepticism.

She swallows, the purple splotches on her neck rising and falling. "I had her, and now I don't have her."

I nod along. "She was your best friend."

Mrs. Watkins bites down hard on her pale, thin lower lip. "She's gone. But I'm not alone." She shudders. "The flowers are everywhere. I'm never alone."

Mrs. Watkins's front lawn was pretty bare. As far as I can tell, Great-Aunt Florence's yard has more flowers than the rest of the street combined.

Had Mrs. Watkins been visiting the mansion by herself?

I watch her expectantly, waiting for more. As though

she's lost her train of thought, she raises the tea to her lips again and takes a deep gulp. Then she releases the cup and it falls onto the table, spilling liquid across the wooden surface.

"Cold," she says again, smacking her lips in disgust.

Jacob clears his throat. "What *truth*?"

She presses her fingers to her temples and sways in her seat. "Since she died, her yard is filled with flowers. And they whisper to me. They say, *we are weeds, we are weeds*."

Jacob's jaw hangs. "Your truth-telling source is the *flowers*?"

I lean forward in my chair, ignoring him. "You don't trust that landscaper either, do you?"

Her swaying picks up pace, so she's practically rocking in her seat. "Their roots are crawling through. The street is infested. My house is infested. My basement is infested. Everything is filled with *weeds*."

She slaps her palms on the table. I jump and Jacob tightens his grip on the back of my chair.

Her eyes flash up to mine, bleary and bloodshot. "Can't you hear them? Can you hear them growing beneath these very floors, right now?"

Jacob returns his hand to my shoulder. The gesture catches Mrs. Watkins's attention. As she focuses on his hand, her gaze seems to steady. "Florence was all I had. And now . . ."

She trails off and thick tears brim in the corner of her

eyes. A dull ache fills my chest. Seeing Mrs. Watkins alone on her side of the table, lower lip quivering, reminds me of lunch in the West Higgins cafeteria. Sitting alone while listening to Ashley laugh at something her friends said, without ever casting a glance my way.

I know what it's like to lose every last friend—along with a sense of control.

Jacob inhales sharply as I reach across the table and place my hand over Mrs. Watkins's. It's cold and leathery beneath my touch, but I don't pull away.

The tears don't dissipate, but the muscles in her jaw relax. "Suddenly she was gone. And now all I have are these weeds."

She clamps her other hand over mine and holds on to me with all of her strength. Her eyes are more focused and determined than I'd seen them as she says, "No one believes an old woman like me. But they might listen to you. Find out what happened to Florence. Make it right."

I squeeze her hand. "I will. I promise."

The mantel clock chimes once to mark the start of the hour. Then it hoots twice.

Jacob shakes my shoulder. "Pepper, we should go."

I slip my hand from hers and follow Jacob toward the door. Mrs. Watkins remains seated at the table, watching us leave with watery eyes.

The sunlight tickles my nose as I step outside. We walk across her lawn toward Jacob's.

"I knew she'd have clues," I whisper, barely containing my excitement.

Jacob gawks. "You call those *clues*? Half of what she said was gibberish."

"What she said about owls and dolphins sounded like gibberish too," I remind him. "But it turned out to be an . . . *alternative* way of expressing her friendship with my great-aunt."

Jacob crinkles his nose. "I don't think we're going to find the murderer by solving Mrs. Watkins's riddles."

I nudge a twig with my shoe as we cross the Buckleys' yard. "Flowers don't talk. But she *was* right to say things have gone dark since Aunt Wendy arrived."

Jacob opens the front door. "But that's *not* what she said." He pauses in the doorway to look back at me. "She said the flowers became weeds after Florence died. She didn't mention Wendy at all."

I get a prickly sensation between my temples. It's like there are too many clues scattered in my head, squirming to find their matching pieces.

"Maybe once we explore the mansion, it will all make sense," I say.

As I follow Jacob through the front door, I peer over my shoulder at Great-Aunt Florence's mansion. Rule number six states that all clues are created equal. Hopefully by the time this case is cracked, I can prove not only that Aunt Wendy killed Florence—but that Mrs. Watkins has more to offer than these neighbors say she does.

RULE EIGHT

Don't cause alarm; pretend you're calm.

At a quarter to three, Aunt Wendy's car pulls out of the driveway and turns down the street. Jacob and I watch from his living room window. Once we're positive the coast is clear, we sprint across the street and up the driveway. Dad's car is gone too, which means he's already left to meet Alanna. Part of me hates him for it, but the detective in me is grateful for the privacy.

In the foyer Jacob takes a moment to look around, mouth hanging open in awe as he takes in the red carpets, grandfather clock, and dining room chandelier.

"I've lived across the street my whole life, but I've never been in here," he says. "This place is even more snobbish than I imagined. No wonder your aunt's willing to kill for this inheritance."

I imagine Aunt Wendy as a girl, as Dad described her,

eyes wide and mouth gaping as she takes in the grand-
ness of the house, just like Jacob is now. She grew up with
Great-Aunt Florence's lifestyle as her compass, guiding her
toward a marriage with Uncle Brandon, and a luxurious
life abroad.

In a way, it's not so different from how I use Mom's book
to guide me through life. I close my eyes and envision Mom
in front of the mirror, preparing for her awards ceremony.
She tells me again about following her instincts, no matter
what anyone else said. About fighting for what she believed
was right.

Over time, I replayed that memory again and again
until the words embroidered themselves in the fabric of
my memories. Aunt Wendy must have done the same with
Great-Aunt Florence, living in this giant, ornate house
each summer. Yet Mom grew up to solve crimes, and Aunt
Wendy grew up to commit them.

It sent a chill down my spine to think of the similari-
ties. Neither Mom nor Aunt Wendy had given up on their
ambitions, and I tried to do the same at West Higgins:
follow my gut, no matter what. Ashley and the other girls
were still furious with me. All I could do was hope my
story would end with me as a hero like Mom and not a
villain like Aunt Wendy.

I tighten my grip on my backpack strap, imagining it's
Mom's hand on my shoulder. I wish, on that day by the

mirror, I'd asked her how she knew it was the right thing to pursue her lead despite her coworkers telling her not to. I wish I had asked her, as she brushed her hands through my hair and recapped her victory, how she knew when to push and when to stop.

"I promise to give you a tour another day," I tell Jacob. "But right now, we only have an hour."

I point down the hallway toward the study door. After yesterday, I'm sure there's an important clue in there. Aunt Wendy completely lost her cool when she found Alanna over there. Either Aunt Wendy is hiding something, or Alanna was looking for something. Whoever's at fault, I'm going to find what was hidden.

As we step inside Great-Aunt Florence's office, a chill swoops through me. I imagine her ghost standing beside us, edging us toward the truth.

The office is fairly small, with a mahogany desk at its center and a tall-backed chair. The walls are lined with dusty bookshelves. The hefty curtains are drawn over the window where I'd spied on Aunt Wendy.

Jacob aims straight for the bookcases and tugs at the spines one by one as though expecting to trigger a secret passageway. I head to the desk and pull open the drawers. There are three on either side, lined up one on top of the other. I start by going through the ones on the right.

The first is stuffed with generic office supplies, from

pencils to staplers. Another holds a half-formed rubber-band ball, surrounded by untangled elastic bands and mismatched paper clips. The next is full of filing folders, and I rifle through them at top speed, finding nothing but old coupons and yellowing birthday cards.

"No trapdoors over here," Jacob announces.

I grit my teeth. Could I have been wrong about the study? Was I wasting my precious time out of Aunt Wendy's grasp?

After I examine the other desk drawers, my gaze fixes on a landline phone on the desk. I shrug off my backpack and rustle through my spy gear until I find my classic detective's magnifying glass.

Jacob watches me with curious eyes. "Can you actually make out fingerprints with that thing?"

"Not exactly," I say, leaning over the desk to get a clear view of the phone. The base is coated in grayish dust. But as I turn my attention to the handset, a hand-shaped gap rests in the center of the dusty sea. "But someone has definitely used this phone in the past couple of days—*after* Great-Aunt Florence's murder."

"So your aunt used the phone. Why do we care?"

"Because old phones like these have callback codes," I say. "It's not as good as the recent-calls list in a cell phone, but at least we'll get one clue out of it."

"The most recent caller."

"Exactly."

Careful to align my hand with the larger imprint left by Aunt Wendy, I lift the handset to my face. The enormous retro phone cups my cheek like a large hand.

Jacob looks up the code on his phone and I dial star-sixty-nine. An electronic voice reads a number back to me. Jacob types it into his phone's notepad as I echo the numbers. Then he reads it back to me as I press the buttons on Great-Aunt Florence's old phone for my outgoing call.

A dull ring fills my ear. Then someone picks up on the other end. I hold the receiver an inch from my face so Jacob can hear.

A peppy female voice answers. "Dr. Morgan's office, how can I help you?"

So the doctor really did call the other day. But why had Aunt Wendy made sure to intercept the message?

I clear my throat, but my voice still comes out small. "Um, my name is Pepper Blouse. My Great-Aunt Florence—"

The woman's voice softens. "She was a patient of Dr. Morgan's for years. She'll be missed here."

Jacob nods me on. "She died of a heart attack?" I say, more of a question than a statement.

The woman hesitates. Jacob leans forward. I tighten my grip on the receiver with no regard for the dust lines. My pulse pounds against the cheap plastic.

I'm about to catch Aunt Wendy in her lie.

But then the woman says, with a self-deprecating laugh, "The HIPAA laws can be so complicated, sometimes I don't know what I'm allowed to say! But yes, your great-aunt did die of a heart attack. I'm sorry for your loss, Pepper. It was unexpected for us as well."

My grip loosens so fast the receiver almost slips from my hand. So she *did* die of a heart attack, and the pause wasn't because the receptionist was concerned I'd been lied to. It was something stupid to do with hippos or whatever.

I remember Jacob's doubt when we first met. Maybe he was right. How could I prove a heart attack was murder?

The office walls rattle as the mansion's front door slams. Jacob's eyes flash.

My dad, I mouth silently.

That's when I hear a familiar clacking carrying down the hall.

The sound knocks the air out of my lungs.

Jacob gulps. "Does your dad wear heels, by any chance?"

My voice is soft as a breath as I say, "Thank you." The woman lets out a sympathetic sigh, mistaking my disappointment for grief.

I slam the phone down. "She must have dropped Andrew off and come back." I search the room for an alternative exit, my head whipping so fast that my mane of hair whacks Jacob in the chin. "We have to get out of here."

The clacking approaches the door—our only way out. My heart rises up into my throat.

"We're *screwed*," Jacob says, pacing in front of the desk. "She's going to kill us, just like she killed your aunt!"

I turn to the window where I spied on Aunt Wendy my first night here. I walk over, plant my foot on the sill, and hoist myself up so I stand, pressed against the glass.

"Get up here and help me remove the screen." The sound of Aunt Wendy's heels draws closer. "Quick!"

Jacob leaps up beside me. I open the window and Jacob pushes the top of the screen, then presses the release tabs. It comes lose beneath his fingers, tumbling into the bush below.

The doorknob turns and I snap the curtains closed. My cheeks puff as I hold my breath. I pray the added cushion of my backpack doesn't make the curtains bulge.

Aunt Wendy enters the room and circles around the desk. The chair squeaks as she lowers her weight into it. She taps her nails against the desk's wooden surface and releases a drawn-out sigh.

Jacob braces himself for the short (but potentially noisy) jump. All his muscles are clenched tight like a fist.

A breeze drifts through, fluttering the curtains. I silently beg Aunt Wendy to ignore it.

Without warning, Jacob takes the leap.

Just as he lands with a rustle into the bush below, the desk phone rings. I hear Aunt Wendy snatch it up.

Jacob stands and reaches out for me. I slip my hands into his and study the ground below, planning the quietest possible jump.

"I don't know what you're talking about," Aunt Wendy is saying. "I haven't called in two days."

The receptionist must have called back when I hung up abruptly. I don't have any more time to waste, so I swallow and take the plunge.

I lose my footing and Jacob steadies me. Then he tugs me down so we're hunched next to the bush, pressed close to the dirt.

"We shouldn't move until she leaves," he says, his voice barely audible.

I nod. Turning forward, I face the house's gutter.

And a narrow window leading into a basement I forgot existed.

I jab my finger against the glass, silently alerting Jacob. We inch forward so our noses are almost touching the old, foggy surface.

For the most part, the basement is an unfurnished laundry room. But a retro green chalkboard positioned beside the rickety wooden stairs catches my attention. What looks like a calendar is scrawled on it in white chalk. The first two rows are nearly empty other than a few markings, but the second two are bursting with notes.

Jacob and I exchange a glance. We don't need words to understand what we're thinking.

As soon as the coast is clear, we're going to find the secret basement and decode that board.

RULE NINE

If someone tells you to stop looking, dig deeper

We wait a few minutes to determine Aunt Wendy's not leaving the study anytime soon. Then Jacob and I crawl on our elbows until we reach the side yard and are clear to sprint around the mansion, toward the front door. Dad's car is still gone, so no one sees us dash inside.

We pass through the main entry, the stairs on our left and kitchen on the right. The door to Great-Aunt Florence's study is at the end of the hall. I haven't explored the other side of the first floor, but it's possible what Aunt Wendy was trying to hide from Alanna—or what Alanna was looking for—wasn't in the study, but a different room in this hallway. Between that and the mysterious chalkboard, it's clear this hall is full of secrets and—hopefully—clues. So, I lead Jacob there, in the opposite direction of the dining and living rooms.

It's hard to imagine Florence living in this huge house all by herself after her husband died. I wish Dad had brought me to visit back when she was alive, like he did over the summers as a kid, so I could have explored the mansion under different circumstances.

We head to the last door at the end of the hall. It opens to what looks like an unoccupied guest bedroom. There's a lonely stillness about the room. Its walls are bare other than a bland still life of a fruit bowl and a nightstand by the bed. As I step inside, my sneakers padding against the old rug, I spot a walker by a closet door.

Jacob presses his fingers to the handles. The walker rolls easily over the worn carpet. "Your great-aunt must have moved into this room once the stairs got to be too much for her."

He's probably right. And if my great-aunt was too old to make it up the stairs, it's not unusual that she'd die of a heart attack. Rich or not, Great-Aunt Florence was old. There's a chance this was a natural death, and all my hunches are just suspicion. Or boredom.

But my gut still tells me to search on.

I open the nightstand's top drawer. It's filled with socks and a pair of pilling slippers. The other drawers are no different, stuffed with faded, rolled-up balls of clothes. All her belongings are practical, leaving behind no sense of who she was or what she loved.

I remember what Dad said at breakfast yesterday, about Great-Aunt Florence removing the items collected on her travels with my great-uncle. Maybe that frame used to hold a relic from their travels instead of a boring fruit painting. Maybe after her husband died, she sold the frame's original art, kind of like Aunt Wendy giving her photographs to Dad. She wanted to forget what she had lost, even if it meant living in a shell of her former life.

Her belongings—both those sold for profit and those remaining—must be worth a good amount if it's worth it to kill for. But the room doesn't show much of her life before, the one Aunt Wendy admired so much.

It reminds me of Aunt Wendy's stiff expressions now compared to the ones in her photos abroad. She, like the house, used to have more color and spirit within her.

It's terrifying to think of how much they lost when the person they loved most left them behind. Especially when I think of Dad's empty ring finger, and of the secret I hold in my heart —the one that could have the ability to change everything.

But it's more than that. Florence's stripped collections, Aunt Wendy's abandoned photographs, Dad's bare finger— these weren't just signs of loss. They were signs of people moving on *without* the person they'd lost. They were signs of giving that person, and their memories, away to avoid the pain.

I tighten my backpack straps until the corner of Mom's book pinches my spine. I remember the family photo Dad carries in his wallet like a final promise.

I've already been left behind twice. I don't know who I'd become if it happened again.

I cross the room, heading to the fruit painting first. Gripping both sides of its dusty frame, I lift it off its hinge. I sway beneath its weight as I lower it to the carpet.

The wall behind it is bare. A disturbed cobweb dangles by the hook.

"Let's try the closet, then," Jacob says.

"Always look for a clue within the clue," I recite from Mom's book. I prop the painting against the wall so the image faces away, then kneel down to undo the back hooks of the frame.

I remove the frame's backboard and peer inside. But it's empty other than the print.

I sigh and reassemble the frame, returning the painting to its spot. I wiggle my shoulders, imagining the feeling of defeat rolling off them, and follow Jacob to the closet.

Jacob hovers beside me as I twist the doorknob and give the door a gentle push. It creaks open to reveal a narrow storage closet.

Jacob sighs. "Nothing."

He sways backward, turning toward the hall, but I catch his elbow. "You're forgetting rule number three."

"When in doubt, assume the butler did it?"

I roll my eyes and tug his sleeve. We shuffle into the closet. "Always assume there are ten more leads you're overlooking."

The sliver of light from the bedroom window illuminates a string dangling from the ceiling, attached to a dusty lightbulb. I point up at it.

"Use that tallness you're always bragging about for the good of humankind."

Jacob huffs, but I spot a smile on his lips as he pulls the cord. The flickering bulb fills the closet with yellow light.

I crouch down to study the old belongings tucked into the corners. There's an empty tote bag, a dirt-crusted pair of geriatric sneakers, and a few pairs of pants and loose blouses dangling from hangers. But no clear murder weapon.

Not that I know what that would even look like. What murder weapon could trigger a heart attack?

"Let's get out of here," Jacob mumbles. "It smells like mothballs."

I press my hands on my knees and push myself up. As I turn to follow him out, two yellow eyes capture my attention.

An owl key chain hangs from a hook on the wall. A rusty house key shares its chain.

I snatch them off the wall and dangle the key between Jacob and me. "They really were good friends."

My voice catches; seeing the key chain abandoned in this closet fills me with a sense of Mrs. Watkins's loneliness after losing her one good friend.

Jacob purses his lips and leans in to study the key. "It's kind of strange she kept her friend's house key in her closet."

"Safety precaution?" I guess. "Because no one would think to look here?"

Jacob shrugs. "Either way, it's not the murder weapon. Let's keep moving."

I nod, but make sure to shove the key in my backpack as we leave.

Back in the hall, we turn to the next-closest door. Jacob and I stand side by side, staring as though our fate rests behind it. There's a bounce in my step as I move forward and twist the knob.

Sure enough, it opens to a set of stairs.

Jacob swallows. "To the secret dungeon."

The basement is faintly lit by what little daylight trickles through the narrow windows. Just like we saw from the backyard, it's empty other than two laundry machines and a chalkboard.

I take the stairs two at a time, ignoring the screeching wooden steps and Jacob's cries for me to slow down. I hop off the final step and approach the chalkboard, thumbs looped tight around my backpack straps.

I read the first two squares; the only ones filled for the

beginning of the month. *Watered flower beds. Trimmed low-hanging tree branches from edge of woods in backyard.*

Each square lists similar landscaping tasks, the pattern suggesting Great-Aunt Florence had the grounds cared for about twice a week. But the squares fill more and more as the month goes on, until there are notes about the landscaper working multiple times a week. Mowing and trimming listed again and again, creating the short grass I crawled through my first night here, so thin that dirt stares up through the cracks of green.

As I step closer to read I spot a bag behind the board. I kneel down and tug the dark green duffel toward me. The sound of clanking metal emanates from inside. I drag the zipper down, and the fabric puckers open to reveal a pile of landscaping tools.

Jacob squints at the board. "Is Wendy tracking the landscaper?"

I press my hand to my chin. "Maybe she keeps calling him here so she can place someone else at the scene of the crime."

Jacob eyes the bag. "Or she's suspicious of him too."

"Wrong," a voice comes from the top of the stairs. "Mom doesn't even know this board exists."

I peer around the chalkboard toward the staircase. Andrew takes the steps one at a time, his palm gliding along the banister as he stares down at us over his nose.

A weary expression crosses Jacob's face. "Ugh, *you.*"

"That's my line," Andrew retorts. "What are you doing down here?"

"It's not just *your* basement," I say, crossing my arms. "Great-Aunt Florence's will hasn't been settled yet, after all."

I add a knowing edge to my words and watch for Andrew's reaction. He crinkles his nose but doesn't react otherwise. After his freak-out when I caught him lying about when he arrived here, I expected a bit more. Especially when alluding to Florence's potentially murder-worthy inheritance.

His reaction—or lack thereof—baffles me.

Jacob gestures at the board. "You've been tracking the landscaper's visits and collecting his tools. Why?"

Andrew shoots him a haughty glance and shrugs. "I'm passionate about curb appeal."

Jacob's nostrils flare and he sends me a look that says, *If you don't take over, I'm going to kill this guy,* so I step forward. "Andrew, we already know the landscaper is stalking the mansion. We've seen the overmowed grass—"

"And he tried to assault Pepper," Jacob says. I shoot him a pointed glance and he crosses his arms. "Or something. But definitely at least *something.*"

"Your chart just proves what we already know," I say, gesturing to the calendar. "It looks like Aunt Florence usually liked the grounds cared for twice a week, but since she's died, this guy—Randy—has been here nonstop. My question is why *you're* so interested in this."

"I'm bored," he snaps. Jacob groans. Andrew huffs and, in a rush, adds, "And I think he has something to do with Aunt Florence's death."

My eyes bug out. I expected an answer, but not such an honest one.

I attempt to regain my composure, to seem surprised. "Wait, you think she was, like, murdered or something?"

Andrew rolls his eyes. "I've seen you sneaking around, jotting stuff into your precious notebook. We both know there's something going on here."

I swallow. "And your mother—"

"Has *nothing* to do with it," he says through gritted teeth. "She has *nothing* to do with it, and I'm going to prove she's innocent."

His jaw is clenched, but there's a flicker of fear in his eyes, as though he's terrified of the alternative if he *can't* prove it. Right now he looks like a small dog, growling to hide how afraid he is.

He's terrified of being left behind too. It sends a rush of sympathy through my chest and almost makes me wish the signs didn't point to Aunt Wendy as the killer. We could focus on Alanna instead.

But Mom told me my loyalty was to the case above all else. If I stop investigating now and it turns out Aunt Wendy's the murderer, she'll not only get away with one crime, but be free to commit more.

Alanna is definitely a suspect, but I can't rule Aunt Wendy out. Even if, in this moment, I wish I could, for my cousin.

I still want to do something to help Andrew through this, so I ask, "Why don't you join us?" Jacob tenses beside me, eyes wide. "We're searching for the same answer. We'll get there faster if we share our clues."

"No way," Andrew says. Jacob relaxes. "I know you guys suspect my mom. I want *nothing* to do with you."

I start to object but stop myself. I understand what it's like to want to protect your mom. I went as far as ganging up on Alanna—even before I had reason to suspect her.

Which reminds me. "Fine. But can you at least tell us if you know anything about your tutor's relationship with the landscaper?"

"They dated for a while," Andrew says. "It's a small town, so I guess Alanna didn't have many options."

I exchange a glance with Jacob. If Randy and Alanna had a relationship, then maybe what we overheard was a lover's quarrel.

Or, perhaps, ex-lovers and ex-accomplices trying to cut ties after pulling off the perfect crime.

"So you think they killed Great-Aunt Florence?"

Andrew shuffles toward the chalkboard. "Inconclusive."

I soften my voice as I ask, "Don't you think your mom has been acting a little . . . *off* since you arrived? I mean, you know her better than me, but she seems on edge."

Andrew kneels in front of the duffel bag and zips it back up. "My dad basically vanished overnight and left us broke and alone, so we had to move into this creepy mansion in this boring town." He glares at me over his shoulder. "So yeah, we're a little *off*."

He pushes the zipped bag behind the board, hidden from plain sight. After a beat of silence, he adds, "You two can leave now."

Jacob opens his mouth to retort, but I place a hand on his arm and nod toward the staircase. With all the distractions, I'd almost forgotten the real reason we came to the mansion today. "We're still not done," I remind him in a whisper.

Jacob scowls but nods, following me up the stairs. I'm not sure how we're going to find physical evidence proving Great-Aunt Florence was murdered, but I'm going to spend the rest of the day trying.

RULE TEN

Respond; don't react.

Jacob and I reenter the left hallway. I close the door to the basement with a soft *click*. It feels like shutting a door on another clue. Staring down the hall, back at all our dead ends, it's like I've failed my mom and Great-Aunt Florence all at once.

"I guess we can go back outside," Jacob says half-heartedly. I glance toward the end of the hall, catching a glimpse through the kitchen window. Already, the sun is setting. We'd spent hours on useless leads. "There were some gardening tools at the edge of the woods. Maybe that landscaper has a toolshed back there."

"Which would be *full* of murder weapons if this was a regular case," I say. "But Great-Aunt Florence died of a heart attack. The doctor's office even confirmed it."

We drag our feet as we shuffle down the hallway, back

toward the main entry. The door to Great-Aunt Florence's study is still shut.

"I was sure we'd find something in this hall," I say, mostly to myself. "You should have seen Aunt Wendy when she caught Alanna. She looked—"

"Guilty?"

"Terrified." The image of Aunt Wendy's face, shiny with a sheen of sweat, fills my mind. It reminds me of Andrew for a second—how he looked when we mentioned Aunt Wendy as a suspect. I shake my head as though shoving the thoughts to the side, and my hair slaps Jacob's shoulder.

He picks one of my curly red hairs from his sleeve. "What was Alanna doing in the study, anyway?"

"She said she was just on her way to the bathroom." As I say it Jacob and I lock eyes, mouths gaping as the pieces fit in our mind. "The bathroom! It's the only room we *haven't* checked!"

"Maybe Alanna was looking for something in there," Jacob says, "or Wendy is hiding something!"

"Or both." I grip his sleeve and tug him along behind me, practically skipping.

We dash into the bathroom and close the door shut behind us. It's a small half-bath with white tiled floors and a shiny porcelain sink. The medicine cabinet is made out of mirrors, and I make eye contact with myself as I lean back against the door to catch my breath.

I drop to my knees in front of the sink and tear open the cabinet doors. "Search every inch," I say, voice bubbling with excitement.

Jacob crinkles his nose as he lifts the tank cover. "When I agreed to help you solve the case, you didn't mention deep toilet diving."

I rummage through half-filled bottles of cleaning product and line them up in front of the cabinet: toilet cleaner, glass cleaner, and disinfectant wipes. "Rule number one, Jacob: *Your loyalty is to the case.* Even above hygiene and personal comfort."

He pulls his collar over his nose as he peers into the toilet. "I don't think I like rule number one."

I twist the caps off each of the bottles and, after opening the tiny window above the sink, drain their contents in search of a hidden clue. But there's nothing but unused cleaner, and the only thing I accomplish is creating blue-and-white streaks along the rim of the sink.

When I look up, I see my reflection staring back at me through the medicine cabinet mirror. I reach up and tear the doors open.

Nail clippers, deodorant, tweezers, a razor. And an orange prescription pill bottle.

"You have service, right? Can you look up . . ." I attempt to pronounce *azathioprine.*

Jacob wanders to my side while typing away at his phone. "It's a pretty common pill for Crohn's disease . . . which is some sort of stomach disorder, according to Wikipedia."

"Can it cause heart attacks?" I ask.

"Nausea and fevers," he reads, "but nothing serious."

I grab the bottle and twist the white cap.

"It's empty," I say.

Jacob's eyebrows furrow. "So either your great-aunt finished her prescription on the exact day of her death, or . . ."

"Someone dumped out the rest of the pills."

Jacob glances between his screen and the bottle. "Why would the killer dump out harmless stomach pills?"

I stare into the empty container as though an answer will appear at the bottom. "Unless they *weren't* harmless."

I place it on the counter and kneel beside the toilet. There's no way to retrieve any pills the killer flushed, but there's a chance not all of them were destroyed. I peer beneath the porcelain bowl. There's nothing immediately visible, so I shimmy between the toilet and sink to peer at the tiles.

"This is officially ridiculous," Jacob says from above me. But I reach nonetheless, my fingertips gliding over the dusty tiles and the divots between them.

I encounter a lot of nastiness—like an old tissue and a hair ball—but it's worth it when my fingers wrap around a smooth, oblong object. I grasp the pill and crawl back out, my hair frizzy around my flushed cheeks.

I hold the glossy yellow gel pill between two fingers. "Does it look like the stomach pill?"

Jacob glances down at his phone and shakes his head. "I have no idea what that is. But whoever tried to destroy it didn't do a good job."

"Maybe it wasn't part of the dumped bottle," I say. "Maybe Aunt Florence dropped it."

"But where is the container for this one? It's not the stomach pills."

My eyes light up. "Maybe the killer *swapped* the pills." I roll the gel pill into the center of my palm. "It doesn't have any markings, though."

"There's no way we'll be able to figure out what it is on our own," Jacob says, slipping his phone back into his pocket.

I shimmy my backpack off my shoulders. Digging through its contents, I pull out a sandwich baggie—or what I like to call an evidence bag.

I release the pill and it plops into the plastic bag. "We'll have to follow up on this later," I say. "But we do know it's possible that her pills were intentionally swapped, and someone tried to hide it."

Jacob peers through the plastic. "And whatever this is somehow triggered her heart attack."

The baggie sways from my fingertips, the pill rolling back and forth with the momentum. I stare, wide-eyed, at the evidence. "Jacob," I say, voice low and thin, "I think we found the murder weapon."

RULE ELEVEN

Sometimes the key is the enemy.

I remain in my room after Jacob leaves, except for a lightning-quick snack run while Aunt Wendy was out of the kitchen. After waiting an hour, I hear the front door open and close. I rush down the stairs and see my dad storm inside. This is my chance to tell him everything I learned and make Aunt Wendy pay for what she did.

When Dad sees me, he holds up a hand to stop me from getting closer. I nearly topple down the steps as I skid to a halt. Was he angry with me for how I acted this morning?

"Go upstairs," he says, voice bubbling with tension. His eyebrows are tight, his expression darker than I've ever seen before. "Pack your things."

I blink fast. "Dad, what's—"

"Go," he says, voice firmer. "I need to talk to your aunt."

He stalks down the hall toward the office. When he's out

of sight, I finish making my way down the stairs and hide behind the grandfather clock to listen.

"Frank," Aunt Wendy's voice drawls, "welcome back."

"You lied," Dad says. He stands by the office door, shoulders squared.

Aunt Wendy releases a shaky laugh. "What are you talking about?"

"Look," he says, voice softening a fraction, "I've been trying to be patient with your moods these past few days"— Aunt Wendy releases a huff—"because I know how much you're going through with Brandon and your move back to the States."

Aunt Wendy shakes her head. There's a strange glint in her eye like a mix of exhaustion and rage. "You have no idea, Frank—"

"You said you arrived the same day we did," Dad says, voice stern. "But you've been here for weeks. You were here when Aunt Florence died."

I clasp my hand over my mouth to stifle a gasp. Dad knows too! Apparently I wasn't the only one Mom's sleuthing skills rubbed off on.

"Who did you get *that* from?" Aunt Wendy asks. "The snooping *tutor*?"

My stomach falls. Dad didn't believe me about the case, but he listened to Alanna.

I close my eyes and conjure the memory of Mom

dressing for her awards ceremony. When she told me not to stop searching for the truth, no matter who pushed back, I never thought it would be my *dad* who wouldn't take me seriously. I had Mom's detective blood coursing through my veins—so why did he believe *Alanna*, a stranger? Just because she's an adult and I'm a kid?

I may be a kid, but I'm *his*. And Mom's.

I'm transported back to the day he mentioned wanting to see other people. Minus the part where he gave me Mom's gift as what I thought was a promise, but was more like a pacifier for a kid he still didn't take seriously.

I want to be angry, or frustrated. But all I feel is scared, as though Dad could slip through my fingers as easily as the ring slid off his.

Aunt Wendy appears beside my dad. Then she raises her finger and points directly at me.

"You always did have a thing for spies," she says. "Including your own daughter."

Dad turns. I step out from behind the clock and offer a weak wave.

He runs a hand through his hair, sending it jutting up straight. "Pepper, go upstairs. Now."

This time I don't object. Even if I'm hurt that Dad believed Alanna over me, I'm just glad the truth will finally be out about Aunt Wendy. I can gloat later, after the case is resolved. We'll leave Maine, leave Alanna, leave the house full of empty frames and broken families. It can be just us, and Mom, like it was meant to be. Like it always has been.

I run up the stairs two at a time, trusting my dad will finish the case I started.

It takes all of ten minutes for me to stuff my clothes into my suitcase and zipper it up. I can't hear anything from downstairs and know better than to test my dad's patience again, so I remain still in my quiet guest room. I fiddle with my phone, wishing it worked so I could tell Jacob the case was basically closed.

After another ten minutes pass, I take out Mom's book and start to jot down the clues I found today. The only missing piece is the landscaper's involvement, but I'm sure the cops will figure it out once Dad and I give our testimonies.

I want to trust Dad, but I'm getting restless. After tucking the *Detective Rulebook* into my backpack and pulling it over my shoulders, I head downstairs.

I'm shocked by how silent it is. I step slowly through the front hallway, listening for a sign of my dad's voice. But there's nothing except the hypnotic ticking of the grandfather clock and the squeak of old floorboards under my feet.

I reach the door to the study and tap my fingertips against its wooden surface. It creaks open, revealing Aunt Wendy at the desk. She's typing on her phone but glances up as I enter.

"Where's Dad?" I ask, hating how unsteady my voice sounds.

She lowers the phone and pushes a folded note over the desk's mahogany surface. "He headed out for a bit."

I reach the desk in an instant, tearing the note open with trembling fingers. I recognize my dad's handwriting, though the words are slanted and the letters almost blend together. It's as if he wrote it in a rush.

Or a panic.

Eight empty words stare up at me from the page. *Gone for a while. Back when I can.*

The words dance on the page, letters forging together as my vision blurs. A knot rises in my throat.

It's him, but it isn't. They're his words, but they're not.

I shake my head. "This doesn't sound right. He wouldn't leave without me."

Aunt Wendy clears her throat, then musters a false grin. "I'm sure he'll return. Eventually."

I back out of the doorway on wobbly legs. Aunt Wendy rises behind the desk. I run down the hall, arms pumping. Her heels clack behind me, the sound picking up in pace. I burst out the front door and stagger down the steps.

Sure enough, Dad's car is gone. There's nothing but an empty spot where it's supposed to be. The sight knocks the air out of my lungs and I stand, suspended in the dark.

Before I can react, Aunt Wendy reaches me. She tugs my backpack and leads me back up the stairs.

"I'm sure your father wouldn't want you running outside by yourself," she says in a too-high voice. I press my sneakers against the welcome mat, but to no avail. I skid through the door. "Even little towns like these aren't as safe as they seem."

She releases me and I topple into the hallway. The front door snaps shut and she leans her back against it. There's a lopsided look to her smile, as though she's losing the energy to maintain it. Her face is pale and slicked with sweat like it was when she caught Alanna in the study.

"Don't worry, Pepper. I'll keep you safe while he's gone." She turns the front lock. The sound echoes against the high ceilings. "Just stay in your room, be quiet, and you'll be okay."

She looks like a puppet whose strings are ready to snap. Somehow, it's even scarier than her screaming. I push myself to my feet and run up the stairs, tears brimming behind my eyes.

What had my aunt done to my dad? And how could I save him now?

RULE TWELVE

Follow every lead and hunch.
They're trying to tell you something.

Every second I waste pacing my room, Dad is in more danger. Who knew where Aunt Wendy had brought him, or what happened? What if the intimidating landscaper was involved? And considering the last person he saw was Alanna, was she somehow involved too?

I don't have a phone or an ally. But I *do* have my backpack. I sit on the edge of the bed and pull Mom's *Detective Rulebook* into my lap. Flipping anxiously through the pages, I scan for something that might help me now.

As the weight of the book settles in my lap, I wonder if Mom would even *want* me to save Dad. While I was carrying the book with me everywhere I went, even when I slept, he had removed his ring. He had met up with Andrew's tutor. Even before he vanished, he had, in a way, left us behind. He didn't listen to my theories about Aunt Wendy but believed Alanna the second she shared information.

Perhaps he had been scared of the truth. Scared that *this* would happen. Maybe he was right. I *should* have left things alone with Aunt Wendy. At least then he'd be here, safe, and I wouldn't be the captive of a killer.

Now he was gone and I had no way to save him. He was gone, and the last thing we'd done was fight.

The last thing I'd done was decide not to trust him with my secret, with the questions I had about Ashley and Tyler Waters and all the muddled junk bubbling at the center of my mind. Now I may never have the chance, and the last thing I said to him was a lie.

Mom's notes blur together. A plump tear plops onto the page. The ink swells in the water, and I anxiously blow to dry it.

I can't damage Mom's book now. Not when I've already lost Dad. I run my finger over the page, pausing on a swirling *S*. I press my fingertip against the letter and pretend its curves wrap around me like an embrace, as if Mom is reaching out to me through the book.

That's when rule eleven catches my eye: *Sometimes the key is the enemy.* In order to get out of this house, I would have to use the enemy against themselves somehow. That was my key to escape.

There's no way to work around Aunt Wendy at this point. But there's one other person in this house—someone snobbish but not diabolical, someone just as desperate to solve this case as I am.

That, I can use.

I tighten my backpack and sneak into the hallway. I peer over the banister for signs of Aunt Wendy. When I don't see anything, I carefully descend. As soon as I reach the first floor, I duck behind the grandfather clock.

From my spying point, I can see the door to Great-Aunt Florence's study is shut. As long as Aunt Wendy doesn't step out while I make my way down the hall, I should be in the clear.

The longer I hesitate, the more likely I am to get caught. So I dart down the main hall, then veer to the left.

The door remains shut, but as I pass, I hear Aunt Wendy on the phone. She sounds distressed, sighing with exasperation between words, her voice quivering with the same mixture of anger and fear she showed when she found Alanna in the study.

I pause, lingering for a moment beside the door. Suspects are more likely to disclose clues in an emotional state. I can't stay long, but I also can't miss an opportunity like this.

"—enough to cover my son's tuition. His semester starts in the fall, so you have to get the court date moved up somehow," she's saying. There's silence, then another huff. "No, I understand that. But Brandon has always paid for— there was no agreement, he just *did*."

The sound of her heels approaches the door. She's probably pacing, but it's enough to jolt me into action. I rush toward the basement.

I raise my hand to knock but think better of it. I let myself in, not wanting to alert Aunt Wendy to my movement.

Andrew sits cross-legged on the concrete floor, eyes fixed on the chalkboard. He rushes to his feet when he sees me at the top of the stairs, gingerly closing the door behind me. "What are you doing in here?"

As I descend I scan the room, searching for something to help me escape the mansion. It looks lonely down here with just Andrew and the chalkboard. He's as dedicated to the case as I am, though for different reasons.

I say, "I thought we could exchange clues."

Andrew snorts. "I already told you, I'm not sharing anything with you."

I ignore him and step deeper into the room. That's when I spot his cell phone resting on the washing machine, unattended. I remember him mentioning planning the perfect prank for Jacob, since he had the numbers of all his former martial arts classmates. If I can distract him long enough, maybe I can contact Jacob.

"I found something earlier," I say, strolling as casually as possible toward the washing machine. "Something big."

Andrew crosses his arms. "I don't need any of your clues. They're all biased against my mom."

I have to bite my tongue not to snap back at him.

But rule number ten reminds me to respond, not react. So I say, "Why don't you be the judge?"

I reach into my backpack and dig out the evidence bag. I hesitate for a moment. Sharing this with Andrew may be enough to distract him from the phone—enough to bust me out of the mansion. But if even a part of him believes his mom is guilty, he may show her the pill to protect her.

Right now, the reward outweighs the risk. Especially when my dad's life is at stake. I hold the baggie in the air between us, dangling it like a string before a cat.

Andrew snatches the bag from me. "What is this?" he asks.

"Some sort of pill." I lean against the washer as he studies the evidence. My fingers brush over his phone screen and it lights up.

"So? Old ladies like Aunt Florence are on tons of pills."

"But there's only one prescription in the cabinet. And it's not that. Which means someone hid whatever bottle this came in. Which is super suspicious." I slump against the washer so I'm eye level with the top of his phone screen. I squint to decipher the smudge left by his finger in the pattern of his lock.

His eyes flash up to mine, and I hold my slumped pose,

trying to look as casual as I can. "Do you know what this is?"

"No idea. It's unmarked."

He frowns. "And you think my mom left it."

"I think the *killer* left it," I say.

Andrew runs a hand over his chin, then turns back to his board. I tap the screen again and make out the smudge. "If I can line up the landscaper's visits with the times Florence refilled her prescription, maybe I can prove he was the one to swap the pills?"

Half listening, I swipe the code and unlock his Android. I find a message sent from Andrew to someone listed as *martial arts jerk*. It's an unanswered text simply reading I'll **get you next time** with an unclean word for donkey at the end.

"Why do you think the landscaper would kill Great-Aunt Florence?" I egg him on, carefully typing into the phone with my body angled away from Andrew.

It's Pepper. HELP.

"Maybe he robbed her," Andrew says, mostly to himself as he studies his board for what must be the hundredth time that day. I can't help but feel a bit guilty for using him like this; just like I'm desperate to save my dad, he's desperate to protect his mom.

The phone buzzes with a reply and I talk as loud as I can to cover the noise. "If he robbed her, he would have done it and left. He wouldn't keep coming back to the crime scene a hundred times a week."

Andrew shoots me a dirty look over his shoulder. "Then how do *you* think he's involved, genius?"

I glance at Jacob's reply. **How do I know this isn't Andrew playing a prank?**

"I don't know," I say hastily. "Maybe he knew he left behind evidence and has been trying to find a way to get back in to fix it."

I don't quite buy it, but it's enough to make Andrew turn back to the board. I text **Owls**, then delete the thread. I can't type any more without Andrew seeing and hope it's enough to convince Jacob I'm who I say I am.

"It has to be him," Andrew mumbles, a sort of strained whisper, as he stares into the chalkboard.

I know I should probably stay and finish talking it through with Andrew. Even though my mom's not around, I've never had to question my memory of her, or who she was when she was alive. I can't imagine what it's like to wonder if my mom is keeping secrets, or what that would mean for me once I found out.

But I have to follow the *Detective Rulebook*. I got what I needed from Andrew, and if I don't move now, he could catch on to me. Or I could miss my chance at escape, and to save Dad and finally clear the air of *our* secrets:

Alanna, Ashley, and everything in between.

Andrew turns to me expectantly. I clear my throat and rise. "I'll let you get back to it."

Before he can reply, I snatch the baggie from his hand and dash up the stairs.

RULE THIRTEEN

A calm mind is a smart one.

Once inside my room, I prop a chair against my door and pull my drapes. After securing the room, I plop onto the bed, springs moaning beneath my weight. The backpack jabs into my spine, and I roll onto my side.

I'm not sure if I should consider texting Jacob a victory or not. I have no idea how he could get me out of this. I'm not even certain he'll try.

It's not that I don't trust Jacob. But he's encountered some pretty dangerous scenarios thanks to my sleuthing habit and has remarked more than once how surprised he is by the stakes. He wants to impress his parents—to prove he's good and brave—but if he risks too much, it might not be worth it in the end.

If that's the case, I can't blame him. I'm lucky I've had a partner at all these past few days. Back at West Higgins, none of my classmates wanted anything to do with sleuthing.

Or me, for that matter.

They got a kick out of it at first. I introduced it as a joke to get a feel for my audience, collecting bets on whether or not Ms. Lawson and Mr. Smithers were having a secret affair. I even made a huge show of somersaulting past the teachers' lounge to sneak a peek at the two sitting close while sharing lunch. Everyone laughed *with* me at that—even Ashley, with that soft chime in her voice.

It was all the fuel I needed to keep gradually introducing my hobby to my classmates. I decided to tackle a bigger case, one that would have real impact.

Though it wasn't the impact I was anticipating.

I noticed Ashley's best friend, Sophie Burns, passing notes to Vanessa. One day, when the lunch bell rang, Sophie stuffed the notes into her pocket and ran for the door. One fluttered down and I snatched it up.

The notes were written sideways and horizontal, wherever they would fit on the tiny, near-invisible scrap of paper. But they all had one thing in common: gossip about Ashley, mocking everything from the way she wore her smooth brown hair in braids down her back to how she failed to pronounce her *S*s against her *T*s without slurring.

I should have crumpled it up and tossed it in the trash. But I saw it as an opportunity to use my detective skills to impress her. In my mind she confronted Sophie and Vanessa, gave some speech about what it meant to be a "real friend," and started inviting *me* to the mall with her after school instead. Sophie and Vanessa vanished from the story, leaving me with Ashley and that laugh that made me blush.

Instead, I walked right up to Ashley's lunch table and smacked it onto the wooden surface like a Post-it note.

Ashley spent the next two periods bawling in a bathroom stall. Each time I knocked, begging her to come back out, she screamed at me to go away. As I left the girls' bathroom, tears budding in my eyes, I silently hoped she never noticed her name written on the wall of the stall.

I found nasty messages written about me by the mirrors in the bathroom the next day, and from the glares Sophie and Vanessa gave me, it didn't take much to solve *that* mystery. For the last three weeks of school, I ate lunch in the stairwell and faked a stomach flu during Field Day.

I ruined everything for rule number one: *Your loyalty is to the case.*

Tugging at a loose thread on my bed quilt, I can't help but think that it's only a matter of time before Jacob gets tired of my sleuthing too.

Then the doorbell rings downstairs.

My heartbeat rises in my throat. He'd have to be insane to walk right up to the front door! I'm wracking my brain for a way to get him out of this when a rock clunks against my window. I peer out into the night and see Jacob in the backyard, one hand clutching a pebble and the other carrying his metal baseball bat.

He gestures for me to come down. I hold up a finger and pull the shades back into place. I can't very well jump down to the first floor, so how am I meant to get out of here?

I slip out of my room and into the hall, tiptoeing toward the stairs. Aunt Wendy is in the foyer, leading a man with dark, wavy hair and his pregnant wife into the dining room.

"I didn't call," she says, voice tense. "But it was sweet of you to bring by your brownies."

Everything clicks in my mind. Jacob must have lied to his parents and said Aunt Wendy asked them over. This is my chance to sneak out unnoticed.

I inch my way down the stairs, keeping low to the ground. Through the railing, I see Aunt Wendy placing a pan in the center of the table. I slip down the remainder of the stairs so I'm positioned behind the clock.

"I'll go get a knife," Aunt Wendy says. Her heels fade into the kitchen.

I hold my breath and run to the door like my life depends on it.

Because it does. And so does my dad's.

I shut it silently behind me and rush into the night.

Jacob waits at the edge of the woods. He holds out his free hand and waves me toward him. I run to his side and he grips my hand, tugging me into the shadows.

We duck behind a tree large enough to hide both of us from view. I hunch over, hands on my knees, gasping for breath. "What's the bat for?" I ask.

He spins it by his side. "In case I had to bust you out."

I straighten up. "You would do that?"

He blinks. "Um, yeah. You're my friend."

The lonely feelings I've had since Dad vanished—perhaps even since Ashley and I stopped talking—dissipate. I stare at the foot of a nearby tree, hoping my hair covers how big my grin is. "I've never had a real friend before."

"Really? You?" Jacob scratches the back of his neck. "You don't seem shy to me. You even befriended Mrs. Watkins!"

"People don't really get the sleuthing," I say. "A lot of them are scared of the truth."

As I say it I think of Andrew. Perhaps I wasn't fair to Ashley. In a way, my sleuthing had really hurt her, just like learning the truth about Aunt Wendy would hurt Andrew.

Thinking about it makes my head feel dark and murky, like the surface of a puddle.

"I don't have a ton of close friends myself," Jacob admits, voice strained. "It's a small town, so I go to class with the same kids I grew up with. I know they don't *mean* to mess up my pronouns, or call me by my deadname, but

I still can't help but get ticked off when they do."

My sleuthing skills kick in. "Your *what*?"

"Deadname. The name I had before. Back when . . ." He works his jaw. "Back when they didn't know my real name, so to speak." As I open my mouth to ask more, he cuts in. "I'm not going to tell you what it was." His shoulders rise to his ears. "It's kind of nice, making friends with someone from out of town. Someone who didn't know me before."

Usually my detective instincts would push me to press more. But everything I need to know about Jacob—the boy loyal enough to answer my call for backup, and brave enough to come to my rescue—is right here in front of me.

"I don't need to know," I tell him. The words feel foreign on my tongue, but also *right*. "You never need to tell me, because it doesn't matter. You're Jacob, and that's what's important to me."

The branches rustle and my muscles go rigid. It's just a passing breeze, but it snaps me into focus.

"We should probably get going," I say. "Aunt Wendy or her accomplice could catch us any minute."

"What's going on, anyway?" Jacob asks. "And where should we go now?"

I scan where the woods meet the backyard and spot the pile of gardening tools Jacob noticed earlier in the day.

I'm not sure what I expect to find here, but so far the landscaper is the only piece I haven't managed to fit into the puzzle. My gut tells me that if I'm going to find my dad, I have to start here.

"Let's keep looking," I say, on instinct. "I'll explain everything on the way."

Jacob points the end of the bat ahead. We head into the woods, our footsteps the only sound in the still nighttime.

RULE FOURTEEN
Trust your gut.

I swear my footsteps sound like a giant's as we creep along the outskirts of the woods. The night is so still that the silence is a physical thing. It's like there's a heavy presence around us that cushions our ears from sound waves. I hold my breath on instinct, hating the way my lungs audibly heave as we trek forward.

I spot a disruption at the edge of the woods. Interrupting the smooth, undisturbed ground is a set of tire marks. Two long trails of uprooted grass and cracked dirt lead into the trees.

I run toward them, Jacob at my heels. I crouch down by the dirt and study the pattern. It was definitely a car, and one that drove through recently.

Jacob presses his hands on his knees and tilts his head down to look. "Are those your dad's tire marks?"

I press my finger against the patterned groove in the dirt. "I don't have his tires memorized."

Jacob frowns. "I thought you were, like, an amateur detective?"

"I am," I say, shooting him a glare, "but it's not in the *Rulebook*."

"Then you should add it."

"I can't add to it. It's my mom's, and it's perfect." I stand, crossing my arms over my chest defiantly as I look up at Jacob.

He holds his hands in front of himself. "No need to get defensive. I just think she'd *want* you to add to it instead of mimicking her."

The thought of writing over Mom's words makes everything inside me feel dark and muddled again. "No. I can't. If I change the book and stop living by her rules, it'll be like she's . . ."

I bite my lower lip to keep the last word from sneaking out. My gaze traces the tracks left by what could be Dad's car.

"We need to get going," I say. "I can't lose him. He's all I have."

Jacob nods, as if unsure what to say after my outburst. I lock my attention on the tire tracks, fingers looped through my backpack straps as I follow them through the dark lines of trees.

I walk between the tracks as though being led by a

hiker's path. The woods are not as silent as the mansion's backyard; I'm greeted by the hum of insects I can't see and the faint rustle of branches overhead. What little moonlight penetrates the thick trees offers limited visibility. Instead it casts eerie shadows, transforming weeds into clawed hands reaching for my ankles, and tree trunks into scowling faces.

I twist my backpack around to my chest and dig for my flashlight. My supplies clink together as I rummage. Jacob taps his foot in the dirt to the beat of each passing second.

At last I draw out my giant retro metal flashlight. Its weight is reassuring in my hands as I hold it in front of me. I press the bulbous rubber button on its side. A stream of yellow light bursts before us, revealing a thick, bulky form.

I clasp my hand over my mouth, and Jacob grabs my arm. As my eyes adjust to the light, I realize it's just a giant rock.

"We're okay," I say, partly to reassure myself. My heart is pounding faster than a hummingbird's.

Jacob maintains his hold on my arm, and we move forward as one solid mass through the dark. Grinding my teeth, I keep from screaming out when a spiderweb tugs at my thick curls. Twigs snap beneath our sneakers, and I pray no one hears us coming. I keep the flashlight tilted down, focused on the guiding tracks.

That's when the light catches metal and bounces back, momentarily blinding us. I blink fast, fighting off the spots in my vision, and see Dad's car parked several feet away.

"Dad!" I cry, making a run toward the car. Jacob tightens his grip on my arm and yanks me back.

"He might not be alone," he reminds me under his breath. "We need to be careful."

I flick off the light, and we're hidden by the darkness. It's hard for me to maintain our sluggish pace as we approach the car. Every nerve in my body buzzes like my skin is full of bees. My eyes start to water at the thought of rescuing my dad.

When we're a step away, Jacob raises the bat in front of us defensively. With my free hand I reach for the door handle.

Empty. And no sign of my dad.

Jacob stops, the bat over his head mid-swing. "There's no one there."

Impatient, I go to the trunk. I turn on the flashlight and press the latch.

The trunk snaps open to reveal a spare tire and a bottle of anti-freeze.

I suck in my cheeks, fighting off disappointment. "We need to search the entire car."

The dirt crunches as Jacob walks up behind me. "Pepper, I don't think—"

"There has to be a clue." I yank at the driver's-side door again. It swings open so fast it bashes my knees. I speak through a wince. "He must have left me a clue. He must have known I would come for him."

I crawl into the driver's seat, waving the light so it covers everything and nothing at the same time. I can't make out anything expect the pounding in my head.

"Pepper."

I pull the lever under the seat, pushing it back as far as it will go. Underneath there's nothing but straw wrappers and loose change.

"There's nothing here. Someone probably drove it out here to get us off track. We should go in case it's a trap."

I open the glove compartment and unfold the map I forced him to grab at the last rest stop on our way to Great-Aunt Florence's. I'd insisted that all good sleuths carry maps, and he didn't complain when I compared each instruction from the GPS to the lines on the crinkled paper landscape. I smooth out the wrinkles, searching for a note, a circled location.

"Come on. We have to get out of here while we still can."

I spin around with my knees digging into the seat cushion to investigate the back seat. My head slams against the roof of the car as I lean up for a better view.

"*Pepper!*"

Two hands grab my elbows, dragging me back. I swing my arms to get free, but I lose my balance. I fall into the front seat, feet dangling out the door. My flashlight slips from my hand and rolls into the dirt.

Jacob kneels in front of me, a stern look on his face. His hands remain on my elbows, though his grip loosens. "We have to go *now*," he says, tone stressed but gentler. "There's no reason your dad would drive his car into the woods and leave it like this. It's a red hearing."

"Red herring," I say, voice faint.

"Red herring," he repeats with a sigh. "That means whoever took your dad knows they're being investigated and did this on purpose to get us off track. If we stay out here much longer, we could be taken too. We can come back tomorrow when it's light out, see if whoever brought the car here left behind any clues. But we're no help to your dad in the dark."

My eyes well with tears. My voice is cracked and wispy. "What if he's hurt? What if for him there *is* no tomorrow, like it was for Great-Aunt Florence?"

What if we never make up? Never have a chance to tell each other our truths, for better or worse?

The lump in my throat is the size of a golf ball, and I stifle a sob.

Jacob's eyebrows furrow. "I doubt your mom's Rulebook says you should ever endanger yourself. Your dad wouldn't want that either."

I tilt my head as a fat tear spills down my cheek. I know Jacob's right, but the thought of leaving my dad out here alone—especially after our fight—wrings my heart.

I nod weakly. Jacob rises and extends a hand. I take it and climb out of the car.

After retrieving my flashlight, we head toward the mansion. The woods no longer seem scary now that there are much worse things to fear.

"Let's meet here tomorrow at noon," Jacob says. "We'll pick up right where we left off."

"Meet up?" I echo. I assumed I'd stay at his place. How could I return to Aunt Wendy's house when I barely got out once?

Jacob stammers. "I—I don't think it'd be a great idea to drag my parents into this any more than I already have. At least not yet."

We duck under a low-hanging branch. "I thought you wanted them to see you solve the case, so they'd be proud of you?"

"Yeah, *after* it's solved. If they knew what I was up to, they'd be furious." He sighs. "I'm sorry. It's just complicated right now."

I kick a pebble across the dirt. "It's fine."

We retrace our steps through the woods, back to the mansion. When we part by the front gate, we're as silent as the night.

RULE FIFTEEN

Don't get caught.

I toss and turn throughout the night, caught in nightmare after nightmare about my dad's fate. In one, we're driving down the dirt road toward Great-Aunt Florence's small town, and the long grass extends from the ground, wrapping around our car like a giant spiderweb. In another, my dad and Mrs. Watkins are trapped in two giant pill bottles, pounding against the plastic and begging for my help. I even dream that my mom shows up, standing outside where Jacob was earlier tonight with his bat. But when I call down to her, the wind catches my voice, and she leaves before she gets to hear what I have to say.

Finally, sunlight streams through my window, and I'm free from the night's terrors. Downstairs, Aunt Wendy plops a stack of pancakes on a plate in front of Andrew. Spotting me in the dining room entryway, her lips curl into a smile. "Join us, Pepper. I made enough for everyone."

Aunt Wendy vanishes into the kitchen. I sit at the opposite end of the table from Andrew, upright and alert with my back as stiff as the chairs.

Andrew cuts his pancakes into uneven bites, his elbows never once brushing the surface of the table. "Why do you always wear that backpack, even when you're sitting?" His tone is more biting than curious.

I shrug and my backpack rubs against the chair's wooden back. "It's a part of me."

Andrew frowns. "There's already enough of you," he mutters, before placing a forkful of food into his mouth.

Aunt Wendy reaches over my shoulder and puts a plate of pancakes in front of me. My gaze bores into it, my muscles rigid as she remains behind me. "Your great-aunt and uncle bought these plates in China. She wanted to sell them along with all their other souvenirs after he died, but your father and I talked her out of it." She smiles down at the plate. "We reminded her it didn't belong just to her and Uncle. We used to eat off these plates together every summer. They were the only expensive souvenir our aunt and uncle let us touch. They're part of *our* memories too. And now they're part of yours."

I make no move for the pancakes, but trace my finger along the rim of the plate. After hearing about all that Great-Aunt Florence gave away, I'm relieved to see *something* was preserved.

The cool china is soothing against my fingertips. Aunt Wendy saving the plates reminds me a bit of how I carry Mom's *Detective Rulebook*. That familiar, confusing feeling bubbles in my chest, but this time I don't fight it down. I'm too relieved that I can reach into the past and touch Great-Aunt Florence's memories like this.

I'm too relieved that, for once, someone lost isn't really *gone*.

Aunt Wendy places a hand in my hair, and I brace myself for another comment about my unruly curls. But when she speaks, her voice is softer than I've ever heard it. "I know you must be worried about your father. We had a siblings' tiff, but I'm sure he'll be back as soon as he's calmed down." She strokes my hair gently, so her fingers don't catch in my curls. "He loves you too much to stay away for long."

Somehow, despite everything, her voice is soothing. Some naive part of me wants to forget about the suspicious note and the car hidden in the woods. Wants to believe this is all a sibling misunderstanding.

Maybe Aunt Wendy was saying this not only for me, but for herself. Maybe she's scared for her brother. Maybe she needs to believe it too, because she's also afraid to lose more of her family.

It's strange that she managed to dig up the last valuable pieces in the house. But if she really was just after Great-

Aunt Florence's money, wouldn't she have sold them already to pay her lawyer bills, or for Andrew's tutor?

Instead she kept them to preserve her memories from summers with Dad. It didn't align with the actions of a killer. It's the actions of a girl, reaching back through decades to cling to the cool surface of a plate so she could trace her fingers over a memory.

Like a girl carrying a bound notebook in her bag, as though its original owner were watching her back.

I remember rule twenty-two: *Always listen to what is around you, not the assumptions in your head.*

Aunt Wendy releases my hair and turns to Andrew. "I'll start looking for a new tutor, but you're off the hook for the day." She retreats toward the kitchen, but pauses in the doorway to add, "I called Alanna to see if I could resolve things for your sake, but my call went straight to voicemail. It's a bit surprising, but I think she may have already blocked our number."

Andrew and I exchange a glance. Alanna was the last person to see my dad before he vanished. Maybe she had something to do with his disappearance, and hiding his car in the woods to create a false trail.

Or maybe that's what Aunt Wendy wants me to think.

"Aren't you going to eat?" Andrew asks me.

Andrew is probably more interested in solving the murder than saving my dad, however connected the two may be. And he's definitely not going to pursue any leads that involve his mother.

But Alanna going MIA—looking into that is right up his alley.

I stand, the chair screeching against the wooden floor. "Actually, I have to go. I'm going to leave the Alanna side of things to you."

Andrew's eyebrows pinch together. "What do you mean the *Alanna side of things*?" he demands, voice low through clenched teeth. "What other side *is* there?"

"I didn't mean anything by it," I say fast, gripping my backpack straps. "But if you're still looking for clues, Alanna might be somewhere to start."

Andrew doesn't say anything more as I leave the house. But while I dash across the long driveway, I sense eyes digging into me. Andrew watches me from the dining room window as I cross the lawn.

Through the gates I spot an unusual number of cars outside Jacob's house. I slow my pace, watching as a young couple carries a pink box and three helium balloons to the front door. His parents must be having some kind of party. I feel bad for drawing him away but remind myself my dad's safety is my priority.

And, even beyond that, I need to talk to my friend. For the first time, I'm truly confused. There's no way to prove whether or not Aunt Wendy's innocent without solving the case.

And for that, I need Jacob.

The woods are less horror movie and more fairy tale in the daylight, with birds chirping overhead and the luscious colors of weeds and flowers visible in the day. Uninhibited by fear, I arrive at my dad's car within a minute. I settle onto the car's hood and wait for Jacob to arrive.

Sitting still is practically impossible. Fragments of my nightmares swarm in my mind, reminding me of all the terrible things that could be happening to my dad. I hunch over, holding my head between my knees. The sounds of the woods fade. All I hear is the pounding of my heart. I inhale steadily through my nostrils, trying to calm myself.

Rule thirteen: *A calm mind is a smart one.*

Thinking of Mom's rules reminds me of the dream, how she appeared outside my window like a living version of the woman in my photo gallery. This isn't just about saving Dad. It's about living up to Mom's legacy, too, and showing Dad that it's something we need to preserve, no matter who else we meet, or what else happens.

If I fail this mission, I'm losing *both* of them.

Time moves exponentially slower, each minute lasting longer than the previous. Eventually I pull out my phone, which—

though it still doesn't have service—can at least tell me the time.

It's already one. Jacob said he'd be here at noon. Where is he?

I clench my fist around the phone. I can't lose Jacob. He's my only ally. Without him, my dad doesn't stand a chance.

A twig snaps a few yards to my right. I hop off the car, relief rushing through me with a surge of warmth.

"Jacob?" I call.

No answer.

I swallow. "Jacob . . . ?"

There's movement by a fat tree trunk. Five fingers curl around the bark as a small form slowly emerges.

I squint, cupping my hand over my eyes. "Andrew?"

He slips around the tree, revealing himself in the daylight. His jaw is squared and his shoulders are tense. He looks like a cat ready to pounce.

"What are you doing here?" he asks through bared teeth.

I let out a high laugh. "What are *you* doing here?"

"Following you, obviously."

Maybe Andrew was desperate for clues. But the way he stands, muscles wound tight and eyes flashing, I have a feeling he's not here for another clue swap.

"I figured out that much," I say. My eyes flicker between him and the car. I take a step forward. "Do you know who left the car here? Or where they're really keeping my dad?"

"Stop saying *they*," he says, nostrils flaring. "I know you mean the landscaper and my mom. And you're wrong. I'm going to prove that you're *wrong*."

His voice is louder than I've ever heard. Suddenly all the stories about his temper seem so much more real.

"Do you know where Jacob is?" I ask, low.

Andrew gawks. "Why would I care where *that* jerk was?"

The woods behind him are still. No sign of Jacob approaching. If Andrew didn't stop him, then where is he? I could really use my partner right about now.

Andrew crosses the patch of dirt so he stands in front of me. "I want you to go home," he says, "and quit the case."

I glare straight into his eyes. "If you're so sure your mom is innocent, why should I quit?"

"I know you're out to get her. I wouldn't put it past you to make up clues just to get her in trouble." His chin trembles. "Things are bad enough as it is without you making stuff up."

Seeing his composure slip, I wish my clues *were* made up. Andrew may be prickly, but I would be too, if someone tried to get between my mom and me. In a way, I hadn't been much different when I'd lashed out at Alanna, wanting to drive her away from hurting my parents and me.

But I didn't lie about any clues, and no matter what answer I discover, it's my duty as a detective to reveal the truth. "I'm not making anything up. I would *never* make anything up!"

"I know my mom!" he screams. "She's telling the truth!"

"Do you really believe that?" My tone is challenging, but part of me is genuinely curious. At this point, I hardly know what to believe myself.

I spot a flicker of fear in his eyes. He's not sure if he believes her yet either. And for some reason, at this very moment, that seems worse.

"What else is in that backpack, anyway?" He steps forward. "Let me see."

I shove past him. For a second I think I'm in the clear. Then he grasps at my backpack and gets hold of one of the pockets, using it to yank me toward him with so much force I topple backward. Losing my footing, I fall against Andrew and we both tumble into the dirt.

"You're writing lies about my mom in that book, aren't you?" I roll off him, but he doesn't let go of the backpack. I clutch my straps so tight, my nails dig into the skin of my palms. "If my mom goes to jail because of your lies, I won't have *anything*!"

My grip slips. He yanks the backpack off my shoulders.

Andrew jumps to his feet and dashes toward the house. Watching him take off with my backpack is like having Mom kidnapped before my eyes, just like Dad was.

That's why I don't hesitate to tackle him straight into a bush.

Andrew screams as we're swallowed by sharp branches and pointed leaves, tangled in each other's grip.

"Give it back!"

He swings his arm, and his elbow smashes into my gut. A surge of nausea sweeps through me, accompanied by a throbbing pain. I slump into the dirt.

Free from my grip, Andrew steps out of the bush and dusts a twig from his sleeve. He hangs the bag in the air between us, giving it a shake. "Whatever *lies* you've made about my mom, I'm going to destroy."

I feel small and weak, lying in the dirt with my arms wrapped around my throbbing stomach. But in a faint voice, I manage to say, "They might not be lies."

The blood drains from Andrew's cheeks. That look of fear returns, and his eyes gloss over as if he could burst into tears. If Aunt Wendy *is* guilty, I'm not sure what that will mean for Andrew. If Aunt Wendy goes to jail, he'd probably be back in his dad's custody. But after overhearing Aunt Wendy's conversation with her lawyer, it doesn't seem like his dad is interested in doing more than the bare, court-ordered minimum. I doubt he'd want to take Andrew back, or that Andrew would *want* to go back after being abandoned.

With my backpack—and Mom's book—in his hands, I almost understand what he must be feeling. The thought makes my already-aching stomach squeeze with confused discomfort.

Before his tears spill, Andrew turns on his heel and sprints off through the woods. My backpack vanishes from view with him.

But I don't move, don't try to get up. I just lie there and let the sobs wrack my body.

RULE SIXTEEN

Always know everyone's weakness, whether friend or foe.

When I leave the woods, I don't head to the mansion. At this point Andrew's probably read the *Detective Rulebook* and my case notes. He has the pill, too—my biggest piece of evidence. Perhaps he's even passed all of it along to his mom.

Instead I go to Jacob's house. With dirt on my cheeks, scrapes on my knees, and half a bush stuck in my curls, I walk past his guests' cars, up to his front door, and knock.

The sounds of laughter and clinking silverware carry outside as I wait on the doorstep. After a moment his mother opens the door, still calling out to someone at the party and laughing, before turning her attention to me.

Her eyes nearly bug out of her head when she sees the state I'm in. "Oh my God!"

I don't waste a second. "Can I see Jacob?"

Concern flickers in her eyes. "Are you okay, hon?"

I nod. "I just want to talk to Jacob. Is he here?"

I pray she'll say no. That he didn't ditch me for pink balloons and sheet cake.

But she calls over her shoulder, "Jacob! Your friend is here."

A guest walks up and asks Mrs. Buckley where the bathroom is. She vanishes from the doorway.

That's when Jacob appears, biting his lip and staring at his dress shoes as he braces himself for confrontation. He's wearing a button-up and slacks, looking neater and more polished than I've ever seen him. Not a single curl is out of place on top of his head.

I cross my arms and glare, waiting until he looks up and meets me square in the eye. When he does, his eyes widen and his lips part on a silent gasp.

"What happened?" He reaches for my arm and I pull it back.

"Andrew happened," I say, not bothering to mask the biting tone in my voice. "He stole my backpack."

Jacob looks me up and down and furrows his brow. "*Andrew* did this?" He glares over my shoulder, toward Great-Aunt Florence's place. "Let's go."

He balls his fist and makes to move past me. I press my hand against his chest and shove. "I'm not angry at Andrew. I'm angry at *you*."

He blinks. "Wait, what?"

I square my shoulders and stand up as tall as I can. "I expect Andrew to be a jerk. But I was counting on you to be there. You're supposed to be my *friend*."

"I am!" he says, hurt in his eyes. "But I have to be there for my family, too. Today's my mom's baby shower. If I hadn't been there—"

"But you told me to meet you," I say, raising my voice in an attempt to fight off tears.

He runs his hands over his head. "I don't know. You were freaking out yesterday, and I said a lot of stuff just to—"

"Of course I'm freaking out!" I point to my twig-infested head. "Look what's happening."

He gestures into his house. "This is happening too. And you have no idea what I'm going through with this baby stuff." His voice drops to a whisper. "I'm terrified that if I'm not the perfect son . . . my parents are going to regret having a son at all. You can never, *ever* have any idea what that's like."

He was right. I could never have any idea what Jacob was going through with his family right now, or in general. There were challenges he had to face every day that I barely understood until I met him—challenges I scrolled past on message boards in search of my own answers. No matter how upset I was, I had to understand that.

"I know. And I'm sorry." I swallow. "But at least you still

have parents to worry about impressing. Right now, I have no one."

A woman with another giant pink box climbs the front steps, mumbling "Excuse me" as she shoulders past us. She blocks Jacob from my view, and I take the opportunity to leave. I'm not sure where to go, but I know, at least, that I don't belong here.

RULE SEVENTEEN
Your greatest ally is the truth.

Dad's car is the closest thing I have to a home, and no more dangerous than anywhere else in town, so I head there. I follow the tire marks, careful not to corrupt the evidence with my footprints. The trail vanishes at times, concealed by rocks or uneven patches of grass and weeds. I use the pattern of cracked twigs as my guide.

My heart throbs when I remember these tracks lead to nothing—just an empty spot where the kidnappers want me to think my dad is. I don't have any more idea where he was actually taken than I know how Great-Aunt Florence was murdered.

And now, without the *Detective Rulebook*, I'm more stuck than ever.

As I approach the car, I hear a gruff male voice in the distance. I slow my pace, creeping from tree to tree as I approach. At one of the trees closest to the car I pause, aligning my body with the trunk so I won't be spotted. Cupping the bark in my hands I peer around the trunk to see the landscaper, Randy, pacing by my dad's car as he barks at someone on the phone.

"—still here," he's saying. "If someone'd called the cops, they'd be all over this by now." There's silence for a moment as Randy listens. "He's nowhere near here. We're covered."

He turns on his heel, pacing back toward me. I duck low, bark scraping my cheek as I keep close to the tree.

"I'm keeping him at the hideout until we know he'll keep his mouth shut," he says. "If you weren't cut out for this, you shouldn't have started it in the first place."

Now I'm certain Randy was involved. But who was his accomplice? Both Aunt Wendy and Alanna had access to Great-Aunt Florence's pills. And both of them would feel guilty for involving my dad.

"My buddy's coming by to do a final check on the duplicate today," Randy continues. He listens for a beat, then lets out an impatient huff. "*Codicil*, not duplicate. I know the difference. As long as the old lady's estate lawyer doesn't, I don't care. I just want to move on and leave this mess behind." I scratch the side of my head. It was like he was talking in code. I wish I had my book or my phone to jot the words down so I could try to decipher them later. All I have now is a faulty memory.

"No, don't destroy the doc yet," he says. "My guy needs it to make sure we didn't miss anything. Seriously, if there's anywhere they're going to catch us, it's *here*."

Destroy the doc. Doc as in doctor? Did Great-Aunt Florence's doctor suspect her heart attack had been triggered?

But he had also mentioned an original and a duplicate. Unless this landscaper was a mad scientist studying cloning, he probably wasn't duplicating Great-Aunt Florence's doctor. So it must be some kind of document.

Had the murderer left a paper trail somehow?

Randy ends the call and shoves the phone in his pocket. He heads back through the woods. I twist myself out of his view and remain so still I barely breathe. I don't relax until it's been minutes since I've heard his footsteps.

The landscaper's words swarm in my mind, bumping against the other clues I'm certain of. Perhaps if I can reach this document—the original one—before anyone can destroy it, I'll have a leg up on the murderer. But that would require not only finding it, but knowing what *it* is.

Always look for the omen in the omitted, as Mom wrote.

I search the nearby woods until the sun starts to set, then return to Dad's car. I slip into the front seat and manually lock all the doors from the inside. My throat burns, dry and in desperate need of water. My stomach audibly grumbles, and when I press my hand against it, I can feel the vibration.

If I were a Disney princess, this would be when the wood-land creatures would bring me a sandwich and a bottle of Poland Spring. Through the window I spot a raccoon bum-bling through the night, long nails digging into the ground, and know I'm not getting any help in that department. I swallow and pretend it's a gulp of ice water.

I wonder if Mom had ever felt this powerless during an investigation. I wonder if she ever doubted her hunch, doubted when to push and when to let go. I wonder if she ever took a wrong turn or made a—potentially fatal—mistake in her investigation.

Perhaps there was something about it in the book. Not that that was any use to me now.

Slumping against the passenger seat's soft cushion, I take a long, deep breath. I can almost make out Dad's famil-iar scent: the soft smell of old books combined with the light fragrance of fabric softener. I close my eyes and inhale, pretending he's here with me and that I'm not alone as the world goes dark around me.

RULE EIGHTEEN

When in doubt, dish it out.

'm woken by banging on the car door window. I rub sleepiness from my eyes as Andrew glares at me through the glass. When our eyes meet, he pounds his fist on it once more.

"Give me a second," I snap, irritable from lack of sleep. And food. And water. I shove the door open, not apologizing when it slams him in the shin and he doubles over with a whine. "What do you want now?"

He rubs his shin. "I know how Great-Aunt Florence was murdered."

I never thought I'd be happy to see Andrew—especially after yesterday. But I nearly fall out of the car when he says that. "You know who did it?"

"Not *who*," he says, scratching the back of his head sheepishly, "but *how*."

I'm still beyond furious with him, but am intrigued enough to listen. "Did you show everything to your mom?" I ask, trying to mask the fear in my voice.

Andrew's cheeks pale. "No, I didn't."

It's like confessing some part of him doesn't trust her.

He hurries on to say, "I went to my therapist yesterday and—"

"You realized how evil it is to attack your cousin and steal her bag?"

"I was able to ask someone what that pill was," he finishes. "We have to drive out of town to get to my therapist's office, and she's in this big building with tons of other doctors and specialists. After Mom dropped me off, I went to the pharmacist on the first floor and asked him what it was."

My eyes bug out. "*And?*"

Andrew reaches into his pocket and digs out his phone. He pulls up an open browser tab. Considering the fact that I've been phone-less since I arrived, watching him use a clear signal in the middle of the woods makes my blood boil. But I'm too curious to complain.

He passes the phone to me. The article's header image shows a pile of the yellow gel pills I found in the bathroom. The title refers to them as Vitamin E.

My chest falls. "Aren't vitamins supposed to be *good* for you?"

"This is a huge dosage," he says. "Vitamin E pills of

over 400 IU, whatever that means, can cause heart failure."

I'd already suspected the pill was the murder weapon, but somehow it looks even more sinister as Andrew explains how it was used. The header image suddenly looks like a pile of yellow grenades.

"So the murderer swapped her stomach pills with these vitamins," I say. "Maybe she was too old to tell the difference. Or maybe someone convinced her she was wrong, that it had been yellow all along."

"Alanna has access to the house," Andrew says. "Maybe she swapped the pills as part of a plan with her evil now-ex-boyfriend. They could have broken up after the murder. Maybe *because* of the murder."

I hand him back the phone. "You really think it was your tutor?"

"It's all that makes sense," he says with conviction—as though Aunt Wendy weren't a suspect at all. "Besides, she was one of the last people to see your dad before—"

Something drops inside me. I clench my hand around the driver's door handle.

Andrew sucks in his cheeks. "I'm . . . sorry about your dad."

He says it low and uncertain, as if sincerity were a new and vulnerable thing for him. Somehow, despite everything, I have the urge to giggle. My grip loosens on the handle.

His skin flushes sheepishly and he dodges my gaze as he

adds, "I know what it's like to lose your dad. It *sucks*. But your dad didn't leave you. Probably." He clears his throat and his words double in speed as he concludes with, "Anyway, I'm sure once we solve this, we'll find him."

It's strange enough to be comforted by Andrew, especially after we quite literally attacked each other yesterday. But it feels even stranger knowing that he's not only lost his dad, but—if Aunt Wendy is truly guilty—he's on the verge of losing his mom, too.

Yet he's trying to cheer *me* up. It gives me the odd urge to hug him.

But there's still a square-shaped, polka-dotted reason holding me back. "Can I have my backpack back now?" I ask.

As I say the words I look him up and down. No sign of my backpack. Yet my chest still falls as he says, "I hid that at home. It didn't feel safe to walk around with it in broad daylight, considering it's holding the murder weapon."

"Then we'll go back and get it now," I say sternly.

Twigs snap behind us. I spin around to see Jacob approaching through the woods, from the direction of the mansion. He's carrying a giant water bottle and a piece of sheet cake on a paper plate, covered in plastic wrap. When he sees Andrew, his expression goes dark.

He freezes a few feet from the car. "What's *he* doing here?"

Andrew crosses his arms. "*I'm* working with Pepper on the case now. Your lackluster services are no longer needed."

I shoulder past Andrew and make a beeline for the water. "His delivery services are definitely needed." I know Jacob and I have a lot to talk about, but I don't bother being tactful as I yank the bottle from his hands and chug so fast water streams down my chin.

"Pepper and I need to talk," Jacob says, glaring over my shoulder at Andrew. "So whatever you're doing here, it can wait."

Half the bottle is gone with one gulp. I wipe my chin with my sleeve. "We can go in the car."

Andrew steps in front of the door. "I'm part of this now too." He sounds more whiny than forceful, and it reminds me of that lonely feeling I got when I'd wave to Ashley in the halls and she'd purposefully ignore me. I'd never thought about it before, but Andrew was probably lonely after moving to a new, small town like this. Even if he was traveling most of the year with his parents, never setting down true roots, at least he had them with him, along with the excitement of exploring new places. Great-Aunt Florence's old town in Maine didn't offer him anything.

Other than doubts about his mother, that is. And a tutor who not only failed to hold a candle to the ones he worked with abroad, but who may have also killed his great-aunt.

"Just go sit in the dirt for a minute," Jacob tells him. "I'm sure you'll find the two of you have a lot in common."

He pushes past Andrew and slips into the car. I mouth *sorry* and follow after Jacob.

We settle into the driver and passenger seats. My gaze fixes on the cake, and Jacob hands the plate to me.

"I figured you'd be hungry," he says.

"Thanks." I tear the plastic wrap and scoop the slice up with my bare hands. I take such a large bite I cough on cake crumbs.

He squirms in his seat, crossing his arms tight over his chest and staring ahead through the windshield. "I didn't expect you to replace me so fast."

I speak through a mouthful of cake. "Replace you?"

He scowls. "And with *Andrew* of all people. Why did it have to be *him*?"

"You haven't been replaced," I say. "I could never replace you. You're my best friend."

Jacob shoots me a quick glance before resuming his window-glaring. "Even after yesterday?"

I was pretty upset yesterday about a lot of things. And I threw it all on Jacob, even though he's dealing with problems of his own.

I lower the rest of the cake onto the plate. "You're here now, aren't you?"

He twists in his seat to face me. "I am. And I'm never going to stand you up again. I promise."

Something in my chest wells all the way up to my throat.

After seeing Dad remove his ring, and Aunt Wendy throw away her photos, I needed to hear that. That at least *someone* would never leave me behind. Would always come back for me, no matter what else happened.

"And I promise you can tell me anything, like when you're feeling overwhelmed about your parents and the baby." I poke my finger into the cake, causing it to crumble. "My problems aren't the only ones that matter. You need to tell me when you're upset or scared."

His shoulders rise to his ears. "I'm not always good at that. I've had to deal with so many confusing secrets already. Sometimes I forget it's okay to confide in people."

"Even your therapist?" I ask. "And your community online?"

"That's different," he says, eyes falling to his lap. "They only get to see one side of me: the trans side. But with the people in my day-to-day life . . . I'm scared to open up like that. I feel like I need to prove I have it all together, so no one doubts how well I know myself. So they never doubt the true *me*."

I think of how I ruined Ashley's friendships to solve a mystery. Maybe I'm like Jacob in that way too—trying so hard to prove myself, I sometimes forget to just be me.

But if I don't carry on Mom's legacy, no one else will. So I understand why Jacob feels the need to put up defenses.

"You can trust me. Always." I brush the crumbs off my hands. "How was the shower?"

He shrugs. "It was fine. I know everyone's just excited because it's a baby, only I can't help but be nervous they're only excited because it's a *girl*."

"I'm sure your sister will be great in her own way," I say, "but she can't be great like you. There's only one Jacob Buckley."

His ears turn red. "Thanks." He nods his head toward the back of the car. "So can you tell me why you're teaming up with your attacker? Because if we're all about honesty right now, I already hated that guy before yesterday and now I *despise* him."

I recap everything we discovered about the murder weapon, and Andrew's theories about Alanna and Randy. With every word released I feel lighter. Even if things still feel murky and uncertain, knowing I'm not alone somehow makes it okay.

Jacob stares ahead, knuckles pressed against his chin. "It all fits, but . . . I'm still not sure. Wendy's been stuck in my head as *murderer* since day one, so it's hard to consider another side of the story."

"I feel the same way," I admit. All of her kindness—the moments she laughed with Dad, or clung to Aunt Florence's china—used to feel like the exception, not the rule. But at this point, I don't know what to believe. Or even what I *want* to believe.

"I can't stop Andrew from investigating with us. Especially not when the case involves his mom." I think of the girls from West Higgins and feel a small pang of regret. "How he finds the truth isn't up to me."

Jacob slumps in the seat. "Do I have to be nice to him?"

"You can be as rude as you want, so long as it doesn't get in the way of the investigation."

He perks up a bit at that, and I can't help but laugh.

"All right," he says, rolling up his sleeves, "let's do this."

We climb out of the car. Andrew sits at the foot of a tree, poking at a patch of clover. He jumps up when he sees us.

"Now what?" he asks, brushing dirt off his pants.

Jacob crosses his arms and walks right up to him. "Now we set some ground rules."

I roll my eyes. "So it begins."

Jacob holds up his fingers with each point. "One, everything you hear, see, or learn while spying with us is confidential and cannot be shared with anyone. Especially your mother."

Andrew signals with his hand for Jacob to hurry up. "Yeah, yeah. I get it, okay?"

"Two," Jacob says over him, "your loyalty is to the truth, nothing and *no one* else. Any leads you discover will be pursued, even if they incriminate your mom. And three"—he takes a step closer—"if you're going to work with us, you have to apologize to Pepper."

"For what?" Andrew asks, voice shrill. "She's the one framing my mom!"

"And *you're* the one who threw her into a bush instead of talking about it." Jacob crosses his arms defiantly. "Apologize, or you're out."

I'd be okay with letting Andrew off the hook, considering the stress he's under. And the fact that I was, technically, the one who threw *him* into a bush. But I'm not about to defy Jacob when he needs my support. So I cross my arms too, and stand straight beside him.

Andrew's shoulders sag. "Fine. I'm sorry I stole your backpack."

Jacob raises an eyebrow. "And?"

"And I won't do it again?"

"Or I'll put you in another grappling hold," Jacob says with a smirk.

"We can bicker after we save my dad," I say, stepping between the two. "Right now we need to find whatever documents Randy is hiding."

Jacob tilts his head. "Document? Like a will?"

A will—of course! I try not to hide my surprise, as if I'd thought of it myself, and give him a curt nod. "I overheard Randy mention a document that he's making a duplicate of." Jumping on Jacob's idea, I say, "Maybe it's a fake will!"

A grin sweeps across Jacob's face. He uncrosses his

arms and gives my shoulder a gentle nudge. "You did it, detective. You found a clue without your mom's book."

The colors and sounds of the woods dissipate. He looks away just after he says it, shooting some snide remark at Andrew, but I don't move. I'm stuck in a haze, retracing last night's steps in my mind.

Was I really just as good of a detective without Mom's book? Sure, I always said detective skills ran in my blood. But if I didn't need her book to guide me anymore, did that mean I no longer needed *her*?

"The last time I saw my dad, I was fighting with him," I say, catching the boys off guard. They stop their arguing and turn their curious gazes to me. "I was upset he took off his ring, and he wanted to explain it. I wouldn't let him."

In a way, it was almost like holding on to Mom's memory too tight made him slip away. Not only had I lashed out about Alanna, but I had kept my secret from him. Instead, I fantasized about how Mom would help me navigate the Ashley crush without my even giving Dad a chance.

My throat rattles like a loose pipe and I swallow. "I have to rescue him and hear him out."

Andrew throws up his hands. "Then let's go already. You're the one dragging your feet."

I nod and we tromp through the woods, toward the mansion. Jacob gives me a soft pat on the shoulder, but otherwise we walk in silence.

I'm not sure if working without the *Rulebook* is the right thing to do, or if I'll ever be half the detective Mom was. I'm not even sure what it would mean if I *was*, or if I'd end up being even better. But either way, I need to focus on my dad right now. Because more than anyone, he's the person who currently needs me the most.

RULE NINETEEN

When you think you've reached the end, push ten more yards.

E ven though I overheard Randy practically admit the car was bait to send any investigations off track, I can't help but feel guilty as I leave it behind in the woods. It's like I'm abandoning some part of my dad. But I know the only way to save him is to move on and find a real lead. Andrew tells Jacob and me that Aunt Wendy was getting ready to drive into the city to meet her divorce lawyer when he left, and won't be back for at least another hour. So we return to the mansion and reconvene in the basement.

Andrew's board is fuller than when I last saw it. He's added notes listing his tutoring sessions with Alanna. He's also marked the day she turned off her phone. I wish he'd marked the times Aunt Wendy left under the guise of meeting her divorce lawyer—just in case it was Randy, or someone else, she was meeting instead.

Andrew stands in front of the board, running his fingers over his chin like an old philosopher. Jacob stands beside him with his arms crossed.

"At this point it's not a question of whether the landscaper was involved," I say, walking right up to the board, "but rather, where his hideout is. And where he's hiding both the real and fake wills."

"And who his accomplice was," Jacob adds. Andrew shoots him a glare.

"*If* he has one," Andrew says. "Whoever is working with him might not be doing so willingly."

I nod. "I recorded him fighting with Alanna, and it didn't sound like she wanted to be involved with him anymore."

And then Dad met up with her, and then her phone went off and Dad vanished. Or maybe it's that after he argued with Aunt Wendy, he vanished. Or both.

"So, we have the murder weapon, we have the motive"—I rub my fingertips together to symbolize money—"but we don't know who did it, or where the fake will is."

I have a nagging feeling like I'm missing something. Or everything all at once. My fingers go for my backpack straps, and I realize what's missing. "Andrew, can I have my backpack now?" I kneel down to look under the board. All I see is the duffel full of gardening tools. "Did you hide it down here?"

Andrew shrugs, nonchalant. "It's upstairs. That's not

important right now. We don't have a lot more time before my mom gets home."

I nod, but my fingertips remain pressed against the empty spot on my shoulder. Even more than missing the bag, I'm surprised I solved so much of the case without it.

"Do you remember anything else from the conversation you overheard in the woods?" Jacob asks. He scratches the back of his neck. "You were the only one who was there," he adds, a trace of guilt in his voice.

His question sounds distant, as though there were a cloud in my mind. How am I supposed to answer sleuthing questions without Mom's book? A dull ache pulses between my temples.

My words sound sluggish as I answer. "He mentioned some word I didn't recognize. Cod-sills, or something like that."

Jacob pats his pockets, then turns to Andrew. "Do you have your phone? We can voice-search to try to find the word."

Andrew, eyes still locked on the board, points a finger in the direction of the washer. His phone rests on the machine's dusty white surface, connected to an old, cracked outlet on the wall. "It's still dead."

Jacob blows a disappointed breath through his lips and returns his attention to the calendar. An attentive silence falls over the room, but I can't concentrate.

"I really need my backpack," I start to say. But Jacob lets out a gasp that drowns out my words and steals Andrew's attention.

"I think I found something," Jacob says. I stand upright and move to his side. He points at the calendar, to the square about a week before Great-Aunt Florence's murder. "The frequency of the visits changed significantly *after* her death, but the *content* of this visit seems strange. He's definitely visiting more often now, for routine stuff like trimming and planting. But the week before her murder . . ."

I read the square. *Fountain statue updated.*

"He installed that dolphin statue," Jacob says. "There was no other non-gardening maintenance done this entire month. It has to mean something."

I nod along to his words. "Mrs. Watkins said something about owls and dolphins being friends. She sees Florence as the dolphin, even though it had only been there for one week of their friendship."

"Maybe she saw something suspicious happen when it was installed, but didn't know how to communicate it?"

Andrew stares ahead, as though transported to a memory. "It didn't take him long to install it. What if it's hollow? What if it's—"

"Where the killers are hiding the real will," I finish, eyes wide. A smile stretches across my cheeks. I turn from the board to my partners. "Guys, I think we found our lead."

RULE TWENTY

Never compromise a case for personal reasons.

I imagine the three of us storming toward the fountain in slow motion as an electric guitar blares in the distance. We walk shoulder to shoulder, arms swinging confidently by our sides and our chins tilted up. Glistening in the center of the driveway is the dolphin, pearly white and vomiting recycled water into the fountain. Instinctively I touch my shoulders, looking to tighten my backpack straps.

Jacob lifts a finger. "Hold on." He jogs across the road to his front lawn and snatches his baseball bat. He waves it over his head as he runs to the gate. "The dolphin is hollow, right? We can smash it."

Andrew reaches for the bat. "I can do it."

Jacob dashes off past Andrew, who follows close at his heels. I don't care who smashes the dolphin; I just need to be the one to catch the will.

Jacob steps right into the fountain, water splashing up around his knees as he positions himself in front of the statue, bat ready to swing. I set one foot into the water. It's warm and kind of green in a foggy, dirty way. Fallen leaves and dead bugs float at the water's surface. Andrew lifts his foot to step in but thinks better of it.

"Step back, Pepper." Jacob holds the bat over his shoulder, prepping to swing. He moves it in mock swings to gauge the distance and point of contact. "Here goes."

He twists the bat far over his shoulder and slams it with all his might. It crashes into the dolphin and sends a series of cracks through its body like twisted spiderwebs.

I bounce on the heels of my wet feet. "You've got it!"

Jacob glances at Andrew. "You want to take a turn?"

Andrew stares into the murky fountain. His cheeks turn the color of the water. "I think you've got it handled."

Jacob smiles to himself and takes another strong swing. The dolphin's spitting head crumbles.

I wade toward it. Peering up on the tips of my toes, I watch the stream of recycled water pour through a pipe that I could only describe as the dolphin's throat. On the other side—in its gut, so to speak—is a plastic tube.

I reach inside the dolphin, ignoring the pinch of the uneven ceramic. My heartbeat quickens as my fingers grasp the tube. Lifting it up, I can see a rolled-up bunch of papers inside.

"We've got it," I say, mostly to myself. "We've actually got it."

I sit on the edge of the fountain and pop the lid off the tube. Jacob sits beside me, bat between his knees, and Andrew hovers behind us. I smooth the papers out and drop the tube so it floats in the fountain.

Last Will and Testament of Florence Blouse.

I bump my knee against Jacob's. "You were right."

I skim the document as fast as I can. It's bogged down with fancy lawyer words and takes me a bit to find what I'm looking for: the recipients of her inheritance.

When I spot the name—yes, just one—my eyes nearly bug out of my head. "Oh my God . . ."

Andrew lets out a rough laugh and starts to pace. "You've got to be kidding me."

"Her entire inheritance, and the house and grounds, go to Mrs. Watkins," I say, eyes glued to the will, "so that she can get proper medical care, a personal nurse, and remain in a place she's comfortable rather than a nursing home."

I drop the will into my lap, clutching it so hard the paper wrinkles. No one from the family will inherit a cent from Great-Aunt Florence. Legally, we shouldn't even be living here, on Mrs. Watkins's property.

"How could she leave us all out?" Andrew asks, eyes staring off into the distance. He turns on his heel and paces in the opposite direction. "We're her *family*. I don't even *know* that woman!"

"Mrs. Watkins was her only friend," I say, slow as I think the reasoning through. I remember how Dad mentioned feeling guilty about never visiting his aunt when he grew up. How when he spoke about his summers here with Aunt Wendy, it seemed more like a daydream than a memory. "After Great-Aunt Florence's husband died, none of us came to visit her. But Mrs. Watkins was there for her like no one else was." I think of my day at Mrs. Watkins's house, the way she snapped into reality just long enough to show her love for her late best friend. "They understood each other."

Andrew spins around, revealing flushed cheeks and watery eyes. "How am I supposed to afford Wolestone Prep without an inheritance? Where are Mom and I supposed to live?"

Jacob kicks at the water, sending a ripple through the fountain. "I think your mom has been asking herself those questions too."

Andrew clenches his fists. "Are you seriously going to push your theory about my mom being a *killer* right now? When my entire future is falling apart?"

The sound of wheels on gravel interrupts him. The landscaping van, with a fresh black window, pulls into the driveway.

I roll up the will and stuff it in my pants. "We have to get out of here."

As I say it, the car parks mere feet from us. I stumble out of the fountain, water sloshing at my heels.

Andrew stands petrified. I grab his wrist as I dash toward the front steps. Half dragging my cousin behind me, Jacob close at my heels with the bat in hand, we sprint through the front door as Randy's footsteps catch up behind us.

The mansion's main hall seems to spin as I enter. I imagine it's full of a thousand doors, each unable to promise true safety. I continue past the grandfather clock, but am unsure where I'm leading us.

The thought of finishing this without Mom drains the blood from my head. The hallway continues to spin. "Where is my book?" I ask, pinching my fingers around Andrew's wrist.

"It's up in my room."

I glance over my shoulder. The front doorknob is turning. In an amateur move, I let my panic take over and forgot to lock the door. Now Randy is too close for me to backtrack to the main stairs.

My gaze shifts to Great-Aunt Florence's study. "When's your mom coming back?"

Panic rises in Andrew's voice. "Soon, I thought. But the city's pretty far from here, so . . . "

The front door swings open. We stand, mouths gaping, as

Randy invites himself inside. We're no different from the dolphin statue: molded in place, ready to be smashed to pieces.

Andrew twists his wrist from my grip and runs down the left hall, toward the basement. I mentally beg him to call the police—that fear of his mother's involvement won't stop him from getting us saved.

The air grows thick as Randy approaches us. His massive form looms over me, and his shadow is a black hole.

Jacob steps in front of me with the bat in his fists. "Don't come any closer!"

Despite my giant hair and the detective blood coursing through my body, I feel smaller than ever. Even Jacob, who bragged about being naturally tall, seems like a lanky twig in front of this man.

Still, Jacob holds his ground. "Lay a finger on us," he starts, voice quivering but hands sturdy as he raises the bat, "and I swear—"

Randy reaches past him and grabs my wrists. I could bend like a paper clip in his enormous palms. His sweaty skin presses against me, and he tugs me toward him. My damp shoes slide easily across the wooden floors. I writhe in his grip, attempting to pry myself free. But he just leans down and scoops me up, flinging me over his back like I'm nothing.

As I take flight and slam against his broad shoulder, so weightless and small, I can't help but wonder if I *am* nothing, compared to this terrible, complicated case.

Below, Jacob slams his bat into the man's side. "Let her *go!*"

He swings at the man again and again. Randy swats the bat and it rolls across the rug. Jacob sways on his heels as though debating whether to run after it or stay here—before realizing neither will result in a winning outcome.

The man carries me down the left hall, toward where Andrew ran. I press my hands against Randy's back, craning my neck upward to catch a glimpse of Jacob.

Right now, he's the only one of us who's truly safe. The only one who can solve the case from the outside. So I scream, "Run!"

But he shakes his head and chases after me, arms extended. He takes my hands in his and gives me a pull. "I'm not leaving you behind. I promised, remember?"

I want to tell him again to run, to call the police. But instead my fingers link through his, grateful to finally have someone that I know, for sure, will not let go.

Jacob fixes his wet heels on the rug and tugs my arms with all his strength. My fingers slip over his palms, and he loses his position to tighten his hold. His pulling does nothing but make it easier for the landscaper to drag both of us to the basement door, as though we're connected like chain links.

He drops me in the doorway, and I nearly topple down the stairs. "After we figure out what to do with you, you're gonna wish you'd never butted your heads into our business."

Jacob jolts up and springs for the door. Randy slams it on him, and Jacob lets out a howl, shaking his banged hand.

The click of the lock echoes in my bones. My hand twists around the handle helplessly as Randy's footsteps vanish into the distance.

RULE TWENTY-ONE
Everything you do, do it for the truth.

Jacob springs into action, taking the stairs two at a time as he rushes down into the basement. "We have to get out of here before they decide to . . ."

His voice trails off. Andrew shifts on the floor by an outlet, his charging cell phone gripped in his shaking hands. "Kill us?"

Jacob ignores him and rushes to the chalkboard. "There's got to be some tool in that duffel bag that can break a lock."

Seed packets spill out as he rummages through the bag. He huffs and tosses a dirty rag over his shoulder.

"Andrew," I say, my voice sounding miles away. "Is it charged? Did you call 911?"

His head hangs as he shakes it *no*. "It's charged, but I don't have service," he says, voice faint. "I had service out in the woods with you earlier. But for some reason, in the house . . ." He falls silent.

Aunt Wendy was the only person in the house after he left. Had she cut off his cell plan? Or used a signal blocker for Great-Aunt Florence's grounds? Unless Alanna or Randy snuck in after she left to meet her divorce lawyer.

My head spins. It's all too much. And none of it fixes our current situation.

Jacob lifts the tools one by one. "We have to close the case so I can get back to my parents. Because otherwise, this was all for nothing."

"It *was* all for nothing," I say, fiddling with the bolted window half-heartedly. Randy said *we*, which meant he was calling his accomplice. He already had the duplicate will, so we have nothing to leverage. Once his backup arrives, he'll need to get rid of the three witnesses—perhaps exactly how Andrew feared. There weren't any tips in the *Detective Rulebook* about breaking out of basements. But then again, I'm going off memory alone, since I've already lost the book. "I like to pretend I can solve crimes, but I'm nothing up against something like this."

Not like Mom. She wasn't just a detective; she was a *cop*. She could solve the case and close it. I may have pieced it all together, but the final picture was too big for an amateur sleuth like me.

And I was going to die for thinking I could.

"We've lost," I say, voice quivering. "We were *always* going to lose."

Jacob crosses the room and grips my shoulders. He leans down, looking me square in the eye with a serious gaze. "No. We *can* do this. We *have* to do this." He raises his eyebrows above his darkened eyes. "This isn't just any mystery. It's about our families. And us."

The empty space where my backpack was feels heavier than carrying it ever did. I squeeze my eyes shut as hot tears threaten their way out. How can I claim Mom's detective skills run in my blood when I can't even protect my dad or my friends, let alone a backpack?

Behind the darkness of my eyelids I try to conjure an image of her in my mind. All I manage is her smiling face from the photo on my phone. Book or not, that's all she's been for years—a face preserved by a photo, while my flawed memory let her dissolve.

"My mom wouldn't have let it get this far," I say. "I'll never be as good of a detective as she was."

"Do you think your mom was born a perfect detective?" Jacob asks. "No one is born the perfect version of themselves."

My voice trembles. "I don't know how I'm supposed to do this without her help."

"Pepper," he says, tone low and soft, "you've *always* done it without her help."

If he's right, it means I don't need my mom as much as I thought. Considering it wrings my stomach like a wet washcloth. If I can do this on my own, how else will I keep her fading memory alive?

But, if Jacob is right, it also means I can solve this case on my own. Without the book or the rules. Or Mom.

Tears threaten their way up my throat, and I bite down hard on my lower lip. I slip my arms around Jacob's midsection and slink into a tight hug. His hands shift from my shoulders to my back as he returns the embrace.

My eyes shut, blocking out the basement. "I can't do it without your help, though. I'm the luckiest amateur detective in the world to have a partner like you. I'm sure your parents already know how special you are . . . but once we solve this together, they'll realize it all over again."

Jacob sniffs softly. As though unsure how to respond, he gives the top of my hair an awkward pat. Despite the fear still gripping my heart, I almost laugh.

"We don't have much time," he reminds me.

As my arms return to my sides, I spot Andrew watching us. When our eyes meet, he quickly turns away.

I exchange a glance with Jacob before walking over to Andrew. I lower myself beside him. "And you," I say. "You've made me a better detective."

He rolls his bloodshot eyes. "Don't lie. It's patronizing."

"I'm not lying," I say. "Before I found out you were on the case, all I cared about was finding the truth, whatever the cost. You've taught me to be kind."

Jacob, who is back to searching through the duffel bag, practically screams, "*What?*"

"He has," I say, shooting him a pointed glare. "I've learned that a case, whether solved or unsolved, has consequences. Even good people are affected by good outcomes."

"That's great and all," Andrew grumbles, "but that doesn't change the fact that if my mom *is* involved, I'll practically be an orphan when all this is done. And that my mom cares more about money than protecting me."

"That's not true." I lift my arm, wrap it around his shoulder. I expect him to withdraw from the touch, but he leans in to the half embrace. "She could be innocent."

He rubs his eye with the back of his hand. "Since when do you defend my mom?"

Jacob's wide eyes ask me the same question. And it's a valid one. I've done everything I can to prove Aunt Wendy killed Great-Aunt Florence. But over the past week I've learned to see Aunt Wendy as more than a suspect. She's my dad's overbearing sister. A girl who idolized her cultured aunt. A woman who married into the life she always wanted, who did whatever she could to see the world, and to show it to her only son. Someone who would hire a tutor with what little money she had just to ensure he had a chance at continuing the private education his father promised to provide before the divorce.

At this point, I don't know what to believe.

Jacob drops a hand trowel on his foot and jumps. "We need to get moving."

I shoot up, nearly tripping over Andrew's legs as I rush to Jacob. "Did you find any useful tools?"

"If you're looking to plant an azalea bush." Metal clatters as he tosses more useless tools around his knees.

I squeeze next to him and reach into the bag. I grab a pair of gardening shears. "These look dangerous."

"Just because they're dangerous doesn't mean they can break a lock."

I close the shears and clench the handle so the metal comes to a sharp point. "But it could shatter a window."

We all turn to face the window. I tighten my grip on the shears and gulp.

Jacob presses his hand between my shoulder blades. "Do it," he says, a smirk slipping across his lips.

I climb on top of the dryer to reach the high, narrow basement window. Gripping the shears by my shoulder, I prepare to smash the glass.

Behind me the basement door bangs open. Our captor growls. "What do you think you're doing?"

As Jacob sprints toward the supply bag to arm himself, I bang the point of the shears against the window. It sends a ripple of cracks through the glass. I stab the crack and the window shatters. Glass cascades down, a waterfall of uneven shards.

I push the rim of uneven glass to make a safe path to crawl through. But by then the landscaper has already reached us.

"You're not going anywhere."

His arms wrap around my midsection like thick metal coils. The shears drop to the ground, but as I'm lifted, I snatch a shard of glass from the sill. It pinches against my clenched palm.

I squirm in Randy's grip, kicking back against his shins to no avail. Andrew watches, trembling head to toe, as I'm carried away. "What are you going to do to her?"

"Andrew, just run!" I say, eyes darting between him and the window.

I grip the glass in my sweaty palm and twist so the point is angled toward me. My hand is unsteady. If I'm not careful, I'll jab myself instead of my attacker.

The man's breath is hot and musky by my ear as he says, "You're coming with me."

Andrew, still visibly shaking, balls his fists by his sides and glares at Randy through watery blue eyes. "Let her go."

I close my eyes and count to three. Then, opening them again, I use what little range I have to raise the shard and stab it backward.

At the same moment, Jacob screams and swings a trowel into the man's knees. "Put her *down!*"

Randy loses his balance. The glass scrapes the side of my thigh, cutting a painful line over my skin.

I release a bloodcurdling howl. White spots clutter my vision like a thousand inflating balloons. I barely feel the man's grip slip as we tumble onto the ground. The glass clatters to the floor by my head. I grip the cut on my leg as though I could will the blood to stay in my body. It seeps through anyway, warm against my fingertips.

From what sounds like a million yards away, Jacob calls my name. The basement spins as I'm hoisted off the ground and dragged away from my attacker, who lies on the floor rubbing his knees.

Randy shouts between labored breaths, "You could have shattered my kneecaps!"

Jacob doesn't stop dragging me until we're on the opposite side of the room. He kneels down and props me up against his chest. "Pepper, can you hear me?"

Andrew appears on my other side. He takes my hand and lifts it from the wound. "It's not too deep. We can make a bandage out of the rags." Seeing my expression, he adds, "The clean ones."

As Andrew ties a clean rag around my thigh, the landscaper rises. "You're not going anywhere now."

Jacob's grip tightens on me. "Hurry up, idiot," he says to Andrew.

Andrew tightens the bandage before knotting. "You can't rush saving a life, idiot."

"Guys," I say, my syllables slow and interrupted by labored breaths. "It's too late."

Randy picks up the trowel and trudges toward us. My gaze flickers between him and the bloodstained bandage on my leg.

Would I be strong enough to survive this? Or just another victim of Great-Aunt Florence's fake will?

Upstairs, a door slams so hard it shakes the walls of the basement. Then a familiar clacking of heels marches toward us.

Aunt Wendy has arrived.

RULE TWENTY-TWO

Always listen to what is around you, not the assumptions in your head.

Her eyes sweep over me, and her trembling lower lip curls. "I never thought . . ." She swallows, the muscles in her neck tightening. "I never thought this would go so far."

Her eyes move past me and fall on Andrew. He steps in front of Jacob and me, hands clenched by his sides.

This. The omitted. Andrew's voice is small and splintery as he asks, "Did you do it, Mom?"

She holds her hands in front of herself. "Honey, whatever they told you, it's a lie." Her watery eyes flicker to Andrew's as though begging his expression to soften. "Please. Believe your mom."

Randy jabs a finger in Aunt Wendy's direction. "Your entire family has left this operation compromised. I can't house every person you expose the truth to!"

My heart skips a beat. Did that mean Dad had been somewhere in the house the entire time?

"What's the truth, Mom?" Andrew asks, tears cracking his words.

"You're right," Aunt Wendy says, running a hand over her eyelids, "this has to stop."

Randy raises his bushy eyebrows. "What do you suggest, exactly? You can't guarantee *six* hostages won't go to the police."

Six? I could think of the three of us and Dad, but who else had Randy kidnapped?

"I know Andrew won't," Aunt Wendy says, dropping to a whisper. "Let him go, give me the codicil, and you'll never see us again."

My blood runs cold. She wanted the fake will after all, which meant that despite everything, she was guilty. Part of me feels vindicated, like I'm experiencing a win. A much larger part of me is terrified. Not only of living with an accomplice to Great-Aunt Florence's murder, but of what this confirmation means for my cousin. I'm too afraid to look at his face.

Andrew glances at Jacob and me. "Mom, we can't leave them. Pepper needs a doctor."

She blinks fast. "Of course, honey." She grabs Andrew's arm and tugs him to her side. "We need to move quickly."

Aunt Wendy drags Andrew behind her, storming to the

stairs. As she argues with Randy, Jacob whispers, "We can't go with her. She basically just admitted to participating in the murder."

I shift my leg, gearing to stand. Pain shoots up my thigh and I grit my teeth. A cold sweat breaks across my forehead. "It's either let him kill us now, or her kill us later. I'll go for the latter."

Jacob wraps his arm underneath mine and helps me to my feet. We stagger after Aunt Wendy.

"I'm not returning the codicil after this," Randy says. "I can't trust you not to go to the cops."

Aunt Wendy ushers Andrew into the hallway. "I don't care," she says with a nonchalant shrug. "I just want you to leave, and to forget all this ever happened."

As Randy stalks off I wish there was a way we could get the codicil *and* have him leave. But I remain silent as Aunt Wendy leads us through the hall and outside, where her car is parked in front of the broken fountain. She hops into the driver's seat, Andrew seated beside her, and starts the engine. I limp into the back seat and Jacob sits beside me.

Aunt Wendy's eyes find mine in the rearview mirror. "I want you kids to forget this ever happened too. We'll get your father, and then we're leaving this all behind."

Jacob and I exchange a glance. I thought we were at the end of the case, but right now, I'm more confused than ever. We drive away from the mansion, Aunt Wendy playing the role of our rescuer. All this time I'd interpreted the clues as pointing to her, but her eyes welled up as she promised Andrew that wasn't true. Was that guilt, or was she telling the truth?

Perhaps the case is far from closed after all. Perhaps it's more complicated than I'd thought.

RULE TWENTY-THREE

Never, ever use the phrase "'Tis nothing but a flesh wound." If you feel inclined to do so, seek immediate medical care.

We soar down the road, dirt lifting like waves on either side of the car. Aunt Wendy breathes heavily and taps her nails against the wheel. Each time we hit a bump, she hisses under her breath, and I let out a yelp of pain, reminded of the literal *stab wound* in my leg.

"Are we getting my Dad first?" I ask through a wince. "Where is Randy keeping him?"

"Your dad is going to be okay," Aunt Wendy says, eyes on the road. "Now that that man's gone, we can get your dad back. On the way to the hospital." As I listen to her promise, there's a tingling sensation at the back of my head. Maybe I'm losing too much blood.

"Mom, you have to tell me the truth," Andrew says. "The *real* truth this time."

Aunt Wendy sucks in an unsteady breath. "I just want us to forget this, okay? You're safe now."

I sit sideways, my injured leg stretched over Jacob's lap. He presses his hand against the bandage to stop the bleeding. "No we're *not*," he says. "We need to get to a hospital."

"But we also need the truth," Andrew says. "Pepper would agree with that. Wouldn't you, Pepper?"

Aunt Wendy stares at me through the rearview mirror. The whites of her eyes are riddled with red, squiggly lines.

I grip the car door handle as we soar over another speed bump. I fight the searing pain and ask, "That man acted like you *shared* the fake will." Gathering my courage, I say, "You've been lying to us."

Aunt Wendy's chin trembles. The whites of her knuckles pop as she tightens her grip on the wheel. Her voice is cracked when she says, "He bribed me. I should have never let them sway me into doing such a terrible thing, but . . . Randy successfully bribed me."

Outside, the suburban neighborhood transforms into the farmland that Dad and I crossed on our way to Aunt Florence's small town.

"Randy came inside for water. He did this often. But this time, he swapped Great-Aunt Florence's pills. I saw him do it and threatened to call the police, but once he told me about the scheme . . ."

"Was Alanna involved?" Andrew asks, voice small.

Aunt Wendy shakes her head. "I was afraid she might find out, with how often she was around the house, and how close she once was with Randy. But no, she wasn't involved."

We head down a rural road I don't recognize. I want to remind her about the hospital, but don't want to interrupt the confession.

"It's been over ten years since I've had to support myself," Aunt Wendy continues, soaring through a stop sign. "My résumé is a joke. I've never even gotten a *first* interview. I was hoping that if we moved in with Aunt Florence, she'd grow to appreciate us. See us as family."

"And write you into the will," I say.

"There was no other way to support Andrew and myself, other than her fortune. When Randy offered me a cut . . . I couldn't refuse." She keeps one hand on the wheel and takes Andrew's in the other. "I did it for *us*. For *you*."

He stares at his lap, tears brimming in his eyes. "You're an accomplice. And you *lied* to me."

"I needed to explain it all to you first. Before you heard it from anyone else. You needed to hear it from me." Her voice swells with emotion. "I'm going to make this right," she says. "I'm not taking the money. And we're going to the police."

Andrew's eyes bug out. "Is that man going to come after us? For revenge?"

"He'll be locked up long before that." She looks back at me. "You have the will, don't you? It's the proof we'll need to get that murderer locked away."

In my struggle to climb into the car, my shirt had shimmied up, revealing the papers stuffed in my pants. I press my hand against the papers. They crinkle beneath my palm.

"I saw the broken dolphin," Aunt Wendy says. "Thank you for retrieving it. Now we can end this once and for all."

She smiles at me. It sends a chill through my body, and I wonder if I'm letting my prejudice against her interrupt the case.

As though reading my mind, she says, "I know I treated you poorly. I did terrible things to keep you from the truth. Tampering with your phone, keeping you trapped inside when you wanted to look for your father . . ."

Jacob lets out a low snarl. I can't help but wince too, reminded of all her *other* crimes.

But I also remember her petting my head at breakfast. Telling me she was worried about Dad too. That she wanted me to use Great-Aunt Florence's china, so I could feel what it was like when she was a kid. To keep that memory alive.

"I thought you would ruin me," she says, voice soft. "But in the end, you saved me, Pepper Blouse."

I squirm uncomfortably in my seat, and another shooting pain darts down my leg. When we reach the hospital, I'll have to give a statement to the police. Aunt Wendy saying I saved her is another way of telling me to lie.

Outside, the sun sets behind the trees. The space between the houses expands as if the land is stretched like dough. I squint into the darkness, searching for a blue *H* sign, for the hospital.

In the front seat, Andrew breaks down in sobs. "I knew you didn't do it, Mom. I knew it!"

Aunt Wendy's story mostly checks out. She agreed to Randy's plan, so she had reason to keep the murder a secret. Even if she hadn't committed it, she still developed the fake will, which accounts for a lot of what I overheard. And just now she rescued us from the landscaper, who would have done who knows what if we were still in his clutches.

Yet the tingling sensation grows at the base of my neck. A few things still didn't add up.

"What about my dad?" I ask, voice quivering slightly as I speak. "Why did he vanish right after his fight with you? And why was his car staged in the woods, like someone had driven it there to keep me off track?"

As I say it aloud, my suspicions grow. So does my voice. "I saw you give Randy a check the second day we arrived. Was that for the landscaping, or for the forger he hired? And if Alanna wasn't involved, how would Randy have known my dad was suspicious without someone else telling him? How would he have gotten ahold of Dad's car keys?"

Aunt Wendy stares at the road ahead. Andrew stiffens beside her.

"You claim *you* walked in on *him*. But the other day I overheard him on the phone when he was checking on my dad's car." Jacob watches me with bright eyes, hands still clasped over my leg. "Randy said, 'If you weren't cut out for this, you shouldn't have started it in the first place.' That means it wasn't him who killed Aunt Florence, but that *he* was the one to walk in on the murder taking place. It means he's part of someone else's operation, someone who organized it all, who *started* it. Someone other than *him*." My mouth feels dry as the words tumble out. "It would *have* to be someone else to plant a fake will, because no one would believe Great-Aunt Florence left everything to a landscaper. He'd need someone close to her to create the fake will, then pay him off afterward."

The words pop into my head and stand, waiting, as though they'd been there all along. So I don't hold them back. Positioning myself upright, I say, "I know that *you* poisoned Great-Aunt Florence. *You* did it, and I'm not going to lie for you! When I give my statement, I'm going to tell the police the truth about what you did."

I search the rearview mirror to meet Aunt Wendy's eyes. She stares ahead at the small expanse of road illuminated by her headlights. The car's speed increases. The scenery flies past, colors blending like dripping paint.

"This isn't the direction to the hospital," Jacob says.

Aunt Wendy scoffs. "Obviously not."

My stomach drops. We weren't on our way to save my dad after all.

We were never on our way to him.

Andrew rips his hand from hers. "Mom, where are we going?"

"Don't worry, honey," she says. "We're both going to be okay. *Everything* is going to be okay."

Andrew's tears of relief turn to ones of fear. He curls in his seat, away from her. "We are *not* okay! Nothing is okay!"

Jacob pounds his fist against Aunt Wendy's seat. "Pull over and let us go!"

She extends her hand into the back seat. "Just give me the will and I'll drop you off at the nearest hospital. Then I'll go get your dad. Okay?"

I press my hand against the papers so hard I'm sure the letters tattoo themselves onto my stomach.

"I'll even include you and your father in my new codicil." Her voice rises, too high-pitched. "Throw in something for Aunt Florence's friendly neighbors, the Buckleys." She wiggles her empty fingers. "If you just hand it over, I'll make sure we're all taken care of."

Jacob watches me, his lips a tight line and brows pinched together. It's a motionless shake of the head.

"We can be a family, like we used to be, back before you

were born." She reaches to pat Andrew's hands, but he remains curled into himself. "It'll be *our* money. Not my husband's, not some random neighbor's. We can travel *together*. Always come back for holidays. And, Pepper, you and Andrew can spend summers here, at the mansion, like your dad and I did." Her hand falls on the divider between her and Andrew. "It'll be how I always wanted it. How it was *meant* to be."

I can almost picture it. Dad and me, standing with Aunt Wendy and Andrew in photos like the ones that Dad carries in his wallet. Aunt Wendy calling Dad to invite him on adventures, the same way she used to when she snuck into his guest room at Great-Aunt Florence's, paper map in her hands. He wouldn't have to wait for rare calls. He wouldn't be lonely, like he is now.

Aunt Florence's memory, preserved. Our family, never forgotten. A legacy kept alive.

I lick my chapped lower lip. A bead of sweat trickles down my temple. "I can't think," I say. "I need air."

"Of course, dear." Aunt Wendy presses a button on her door, and my window rolls down. The wind whips my hair around my cheeks.

After a moment she extends her hand again. "Is that better, hon? Are you thinking clearly now?" Her fingers writhe, stretching back as if they could extend on command.

"Much better," I say. I pull up my shirt and lift the will from my waistband.

The whites of Jacob's eyes flash. "Pepper," he says, low and cautioning.

My fingertip grazes Great-Aunt Florence's name. I press the stack of papers to my chest, close my eyes, and mumble, "I'm sorry."

Then I toss the will out the window.

Aunt Wendy slams on the brakes. The car slides a few feet before coming to a halt. We jolt forward before we're slammed back against our seats by the seat belts. From the rear windshield I watch the pages flap in the wind and spiral backward down the road. They soar apart, wiggling in the breeze as they spin in different directions. Some wander into the farmland, caught in the tall blades of grass. Others brush against the dirt before fluttering farther off. A few are soaked in puddles and float before steadily sinking as they absorb the water.

"What have you *done*?" she shrieks over the squeal of the brakes. "Now *anyone* can find the original! You stupid, stupid *brat*!"

She throws the car into park and leaps out. She pauses to rip her heels off, then breaks into a run.

Ignoring the searing pain in my thigh, I sit up and stretch my hand toward the front seat. "Pass me her phone. This is our only chance to escape."

Andrew digs in her purse, though he shoots me a hesitant glance. "You're going to call the police, aren't you?"

"Of course she is!" Jacob cries. "And don't try to stop her. We shouldn't have to die because your mom—"

"Is going to go to jail," Andrew says. He pulls the phone from her bag, hand shaking. "If you make this phone call, my life is over."

"My life will literally be over if we *don't* make it," I say, pointing to my stab wound. In a softer tone, I add, "Andrew, we don't have time to waste."

Jacob grasps at the phone, and Andrew tugs his arm away. I swear I hear my blood pulsating like the ticking of a clock.

"No matter what happens, you won't be alone," I say. "There may be no Wolestone Prep, or first-class tutors. There may not be trips and beaches and holidays abroad. But my dad and I will take care of you. We'll *love* you. I *promise*."

Andrew inhales sharply, then dials three digits. A female voice echoes through the speaker. "What is your emergency?"

Andrew's voice is fragmented and shaky, but he manages to say, "My cousin was stabbed. She needs an ambulance. And my mom . . ." A tear spills down his cheek. "Just send the police, too, okay?"

As Andrew describes our location to the dispatcher, Jacob squeezes my hand. "It's going to be okay. It'll all be over soon." He smiles. "We did it, Pepper."

I want to let out a whooping cheer, or burst into applause

or a happy dance. But for some reason I feel like an elephant is sitting on my chest and I can barely muster a half-hearted smile.

"Thanks," I say, returning the squeeze, "but my dad is still out there."

I always pictured solving a big case as looking like the photo. Mom beaming beside me, trophy in hand. Perhaps there was more to that case than I could see in a snapshot. Perhaps I had reduced the moment down to a cliché—something small and simple that I could manage, could hold, could carry.

My memories of that day with my mom formed from the photo rather than real moments. I had been too young to clearly remember anything that wasn't preserved within that 8 x 11 frame. Even that time by the mirror, Mom fluffing her hair just like I learned to do mine—even that was just an echo of the photo, another version of the story I told myself to get by.

The only way to unveil the ending was to solve this case of my own—and that meant saving Dad.

RULE TWENTY-FOUR

You're only as good as your partner.

O nce the nurses clear the blood away from my wound and stitch me up, it looks more like a jab than a stab. They tell me I can leave the hospital as soon as a guardian comes to get me. I'm basically stuck until the cops finish searching the mansion.

Andrew is stuck too. He's at the police station where Aunt Wendy's being held, probably sitting under a weighted blanket and pretending not to cry while the police try to get ahold of his dad. He was in so much shock, he went along with the police without a fight. I was bleeding too much for anyone to listen to me, unless I was telling them how many fingers they were holding up. But the last thing Andrew needs right now is for his dad not to show up. Or for his dad to come just to leave again.

I thought I understood Andrew—that we'd experienced

the same thing, me losing my mom and him losing his dad. But if my mom could, she'd be here with me. She'd *choose* me. Uncle Brandon has the choice to answer the officers' calls. To take Andrew back, be a family again. But he'd already chosen to leave Andrew once. And he could choose to leave him again.

I wish I could have kept Andrew with me, like the *Detective Rulebook* or the photo in Dad's pocket, so he felt seen and wanted. I need to find Dad so we can go get Andrew and let him know he still has family that loves him.

I need to find Dad.

Jacob paces at the end of my bed. One of the cops had a nurse call his parents, and they're headed over now.

He glares at the floor and runs a hand through his hair. "When they get here, I'm *so* dead."

"That's not a polite analogy, given the situation," I tease, attempting to lighten the mood.

His expression doesn't soften. "I was sure all of this would make them proud, but the way this ended up, it's like we should have just called the cops in the first place. And that's exactly what they'll say."

"But we couldn't get help until we knew for sure," I remind him. "There's no way they would have believed a couple of middle schoolers that my great-aunt's heart attack was *triggered*."

As I say it two cops bustle into the room with a nurse at

their heels. I swing my legs over the side of the bed, ignoring the shooting pain in my thigh.

"Did you find him?" I ask, my voice higher and younger-sounding than I intended.

The heftier of the two cops clears his throat, knuckles pressed to his lips. "The mansion was empty. We couldn't even find this codicil you mentioned."

When we'd given our statements earlier, the cops recognized Randy's strange term and told us it was a handwritten addition to a will—one that could change who inherited Great-Aunt Florence's property. I remembered Aunt Wendy passing a check to Randy that first day of sleuthing with Jacob and realized she was helping him hire a forgery expert. But when I told the cops, they didn't seem to be listening. Just like they aren't *really* listening to me now. I imagine this must be what Mom felt like when the cops at her precinct wouldn't listen to the clues she'd gathered about the staged robberies.

With her, it was because she was a woman. With me, it's because I'm a kid. But in both cases, we're still right.

The cop scratches the side of his neck. "All in all, there's no evidence that ties the victim's landscaper to this investigation."

Jacob stops pacing. "But we were *there*."

The cop rubs his temple. "Regardless, your father has been gone long enough that it's considered a missing persons case. Do you have anyone to stay with in the meantime?"

My eyes start to well and my lower lip trembles, preventing a reply. Jacob speaks up. "She'll stay with me and my parents."

"We'll keep you informed of any updates," the cop says, then heads out with his partner.

The nurse checks my IV and pats my shoulder as she assures us the Buckleys are on their way. She talks slow in a cutesy voice, drawing out her vowels, like *Yoou all riiiiight? Do you neeeed anythiiiing? You're okaaaaay. It'll be okaaaaaaaaaay.* It reminds me of Aunt Wendy's sugar-sweet voice. I'm grateful when the nurse finally gives up and leaves.

Mrs. Buckley walks down the hospital hallway, headed toward my room. I slump into my pillow and squeeze my eyes shut, mustering all my imaginary power to pretend it's my dad coming for me.

Awkward doesn't begin to describe the ride back to Jacob's house. Jacob and I are crammed in the back seat with my new crutches. We're cleaner than when the EMTs found us, but our clothes are still stained with dirt and blood. Mr. Buckley is fuming, fists clenched around the wheel, and Mrs. Buckley is doing breathing exercises as if she's already in labor. The lectures start and stop. Mr. Buckley chastises Jacob; then Mrs. Buckley places her hand on his thigh and he pauses as if she pressed a button on a remote. Then, after a minute of silent fuming, his lectures resume.

"Your mother is in her third trimester," he says, screeching to a halt at a red light. "She doesn't need this kind of stress. What made you think—"

Mrs. Buckley pats his leg. Her other hand rests on her round belly, rubbing calming circles as though trying to soothe herself (or the baby?) to rest. "Not in front of our guest," she whispers. As if I can't hear.

Mr. Buckley glares at me in the rearview mirror. It's obvious he blames me—Jacob's mysterious new friend—for a large part of this.

Jacob's face is sheet-pale and his entire body is slumped. His voice is unusually small as he says, "We caught a killer, Dad. That's pretty heroic, right?"

He sounds like he's trying to convince his father *and* himself.

"It's *dangerous*," Mr. Buckley says, exasperated. "You're damn lucky you're alive."

"Language," Mrs. Buckley snaps. She presses her fingers to her temples and inhales sharply. "I'm sorry if you've felt left out with the shower and everything else going on. You should have *told* me if you were lonely. You didn't have to . . ."

Now *her* eyes find mine in the mirror. It's as if she's

saying: you didn't have to befriend someone like *that*.

"We'll talk more about this at home," she finishes. I'm sure Mr. Buckley is going to start up again regardless, but then we turn onto our street as though it was summoned by her words.

We're rushed inside and I have a feeling Jacob's parents are impatient to tell him off without a stranger in the room. Mrs. Buckley directs me to the baby's future bedroom, a small space consisting of cardboard boxes and a half-made crib. She lays out a sleeping bag on the floor next to a Costco-size package of diapers and offers me an old nightgown to replace my dirty shirt and shorts. The room is silent other than the creaking of floorboards under her weight. With a mumbled "Good night," she shuts off the light as she leaves.

I lie flat and fully dressed on the sleeping bag and listen for the sound of her receding footsteps. I've already caused the Buckleys enough trouble, but there's no way I can stay still. Not when my dad's still out there.

The case blossomed into much more than I'd planned, and Jacob didn't sign up for that. His motivation had backfired; his parents were *furious* at him for getting involved with me. So even if I was going to cause trouble by sneaking away, I would at least keep Jacob out of it. For not only their sakes, but his as well.

After several minutes, I can still hear the murmur of

Jacob's parents arguing in the living room. I opt for the window.

I pass my crutch through, then my good leg. Leaning my weight on both, I pull myself through the window and onto the soft grass below. The evening breeze rustles my curls as I trudge across the lawn as quietly as I can with one and a half legs (the injured one being the half). Already, a sweat breaks out across my forehead. I ignore it and hobble forward.

Seven feet and what seems like an hour later, a voice calls out from the house, "Watch out for the rosebush, silly."

Jacob leans his elbows against his windowsill, smirking.

Seeing my dumbfounded expression, he says, "I know you well enough by now to assume you weren't going to sit still just because my parents said so."

I want to laugh, but instead I say, "You can't come with me."

"Because my parents said so?"

"Because the only reason you started all this was to impress them. And now they're furious."

"Maybe it started that way," he says. "Maybe now it's about proving it to myself. Showing that I'm cut out for it . . . and I can teach my little sister to be tough." He grins softly. "Like you."

A blush rises in my cheeks. My resolve is melting. "I saw your face in the car. It was like . . . someone had *died* when your parents said all that."

Jacob's eyes flicker down and he shrugs. "Someone might

actually die if we don't do something." My heart sinks at the words, and he quickly adds, in a light tone, "What else am I going to do, anyway? Play *Zelda* and watch Mrs. Watkins pace her living room?"

A confused look crosses his face as he stares past me toward Mrs. Watkins's house. The lawn is dark, but standing by Jacob's window, I'm close enough to see Mrs. Watkins's front lock hanging askew, as though it'd been smashed by a blunt object.

"Do you think she's forgetful enough to break into her own house?" Jacob asks.

The answer forms on my tongue as I speak, as if it had been there, waiting, from the beginning. "Or someone left *his* copy of the key in Great-Aunt Florence's closet, and two pesky sleuths took it as evidence."

We watch, still as the trees' shadows, as a silhouette passes through her living room.

When I overheard Randy in the woods, he mentioned a hideout. But the cops hadn't found any sign of him in the mansion, which meant his fortress lay somewhere else.

Somewhere like Mrs. Watkins's house.

"Rule number twelve," I recite. "Follow every lead and every hunch. They're trying to tell you something. Mrs. Watkins said the weeds had infected her house *after* Great-Aunt Florence died. Maybe it wasn't my basement that Randy used as a hideout. Maybe it's *hers*."

Jacob rolls up his sleeves. "All right. Let's do this. Let's save your dad."

He loosens the screen and climbs out to join me, careful to avoid the rosebush. With my one arm leaning on the crutch and the other looped through his, we head across the grass toward the landscaper's hideout.

WARNING

If you follow these rules and succeed, I will be immensely proud and love you all the more.

I press my fingertips against Mrs. Watkins's broken door and give it a gentle nudge. It creaks open to reveal her living room, shrouded in light. A dozen owl eyes stare back at us.

I hobble through the door. Jacob catches my elbow.

"Randy could be anywhere," he whispers.

"So could my dad," I say.

He releases my arm and follows.

I press my feet daintily against the floorboards as I move forward, careful not to cause a creaky screech. Now that we have to be quiet, Mrs. Watkins's living room seems like a maze; slippers scattered across the floor, spools of yarn undone, and owl displays awkwardly protruding into the walking space. Each of the fake animals' yellow eyes seems to be watching our movements as we trek through the living room, their beaks gaped as though prepared to cry out and alert Randy to trespassers.

The bottom of my crutch squeaks against the floorboard. I freeze.

Suddenly, a loud chime echoes through the house like an alarm.

I stare back at Jacob. He looks like he's going to be sick. My skin burns brighter than my hair.

Then her clock hoots nine times. It wasn't an alarm after all. The house is still. We breathe sighs of relief.

"Is someone there?"

Jacob and I exchange a glance. Mrs. Watkins's whisper came from her dining room. We inch forward.

"Is he back?" comes another voice.

Dad.

I move at double speed, swinging the crutch forward in swooping motions. There, in the space between the dining room and kitchen, is Dad. He's tied to a chair with a thick, black gardening hose. His hair stands up around his head, caked with dirt and a few stray leaves. There are cuts and bruises along his neck and arms, and his glasses are cracked.

My eyes fill with tears at the sight of him. "Dad!"

I prop my crutch against the wall and swing my arms around his shoulders, squeezing his neck as hard as I can. He sputters at the impact, then leans his head forward so his cheek presses against the side of my head.

"Pepper, honey," he says, voice filled with a mixture of relief and fear. "You shouldn't be here."

"We're going to save you," I say, releasing him to point back at Jacob. He offers a weak wave.

Dad's eyebrows furrow. "No, you're going to leave here and call the police. Immediately. If you get caught by this man too, I'll—"

"We've got it under control," I assure him. Dad wouldn't listen to me before, maybe because he wanted to protect his memory of Aunt Wendy, or maybe because he didn't take my hunch seriously, just like Mom's coworkers didn't believe hers. But this was my chance to prove to him that I'd been right all along—that he could trust me to do the right thing. I nod to Jacob, who rushes to my side and works on untying the hose. "I'm solving the case, just like Mom would have."

His expression falls. "Please, Pepper, don't—"

"You see the weeds, now, don't you?"

I'd almost forgotten about the other hostages. Beside Dad, tied by thick rope, are Alanna and Mrs. Watkins.

Mrs. Watkins stomps her slippers on the floorboards. "The weeds are growing beneath us, right now. Do you hear them?"

We fall silent. The soft thump of footsteps carries from under the ground. Randy is in Mrs. Watkins's basement.

I never would have guessed he was so close by from his frequent drives on and off the property in the official landscaping van. But that was probably the point. He'd hid Mrs.

Watkins's keys in Aunt Florence's closet and retrieved them under the guise of landscaping so the neighbors wouldn't pay him mind. He'd returned at night to his hideout without his van, and no one in the cul-de-sac had suspected a thing.

Alanna is breathless as she speaks. "We think he's been using this place as a hideout since your aunt died. He's been planting false evidence to frame Mrs. Watkins in case the doctors found out about the pills." Her chin trembles. "If I hadn't broken up with him, he may have done this at my apartment and framed *me*." She shoots an anxious glance at my dad. "But at least then you wouldn't have been involved."

I get a twisty feeling in my gut, but force myself to ignore it. After all that's happened, my dad's crush on Alanna is currently the least of my concerns.

"This isn't your fault. You couldn't have known about Randy any better than I could have about my . . ." Dad's voice trails off as though he's not ready to say it aloud yet. He swallows hard and says, "We would have been dragged into this mess one way or another."

Jacob returns from the kitchen with a serrated knife. Carefully, he starts on the hose.

Dad hisses under his breath, so quiet I can barely hear, "You need to get out of here. *Now*."

I glance at my crutch. "I can't leave you."

"You have to. Please." His eyes are stern, but his lower lip trembles. "I already lost your mom. I can't lose you, too."

I thought Dad wasn't listening because he didn't take me seriously. Because I was too young to carry on Mom's legacy. To be enough to make our family complete.

I'd never considered how my sleuthing hobby might scare, or even hurt, my dad.

Perhaps keeping secrets was another way of losing each other. Perhaps I already *had* hurt him, and myself, by refusing to talk.

"Pepper," Jacob whispers. He tilts his head toward the front door. "Go call the police. I'll take care of this."

Movement echoes from the main hallway.

Jacob's voice rises. "*Go.*"

I lean on my crutch and hobble toward the entryway to the living room. I peer around the wall. A shadow shifts in the hallway, but Randy hasn't headed our way yet. I rush through the living room as fast (and quietly) as I can.

On my way to the door, I see a spot of white from the corner of my eye. On Mrs. Watkins's coffee table, between her owl vase and ornithology guidebook, rests a stack of papers.

The duplicate will. Randy's copy. The one with the fake codicil.

I stand in the center of the living room as if pulled between the front door and the fake will. The increasing sound of Randy's footsteps helps me justify the decision I planned to make all along.

Ducking behind the couch and stealing the fake will.

I dive onto the floor between the couch and coffee table and shove my crutch beneath the table, out of view. As Randy enters the living room, I reach up and snatch the will. I stuff it in my waistband.

Randy storms past me toward the dining room. My gut twists at the thought of him seeing Jacob, armed with a kitchen knife, and my dad half-untied but still immobile.

I glance at the door. Dad practically begged me to leave. Jacob wants to stall Randy until I can call the cops. Following Mom's rules has gotten me in more trouble than I predicted, but it's also solved a case bigger than any I had ever imagined.

So, I follow one last rule, number nineteen: *When you think you've reached the end, push ten more yards.*

I press my palms against the hardwood floor and push up. With one hand clamped on the edge of the couch cushion, I rise, applying pressure to my good leg. I plant both feet firm on the ground, and blood leaks from my bandage as I steady my balance. I ignore the warm rush it sends down my knee and focus on Randy's broad back.

He hovers by Jacob and the hostages, fists at his sides. He shouts something and swings his arm, knocking over an owl statue. It shatters into a thousand pieces at Dad's ankles.

I need to intervene. I have to stop Randy, once and for all. I glance down at my crutch. It *looks* like a good weapon, but would probably snap in half if I smacked Randy with it. I wrack my brain for some tip left by my mother to help with this moment, but there's nothing. My mind is a blank page.

I grip two handfuls of hair by my temples, scanning the room desperately for a clue. But the scariest thing I see is that hooting clock that terrified us when we arrived.

The clock! It's an old-fashioned mantel clock, basically a block of thick wood carved into an owl shape. And the bluntest object in the room.

I limp toward the fireplace, ignoring the searing pain from my wound. The harder my heart pumps, the less I notice the pain. I lift the clock into my hands, my arms shuddering under the weight.

I cross the room, ducking from shadow to shadow. With my back pressed against the wall, I peer around the corner toward the kitchen. Dad, Alanna, and Mrs. Watkins are staring up at Randy with wide eyes. But Jacob notices me immediately, his gaze flickering to me before quickly returning to Randy. Instantly, Jacob's grip on the knife steadies.

"Take another step and I *will* hurt you," he says, voice inflated with mock confidence.

Randy scoffs. "I think I've heard that line from you before."

The next moment happens in slow motion in my mind.

Randy approaches Jacob and suddenly the clock is feather-light in my hands. I raise it above my head and step forward, the pain in my leg a distant memory. I tilt the clock back before smashing it against Randy's head.

His bulky form collapses with a *thump* by Dad's feet. Jacob drops his knife and it clatters to the ground. We wait to see if Randy will move, suspended in time until we're sure he's unconscious.

Jacob crouches beside Randy and rolls him onto his back. He holds his wrist in front of Randy's mouth and says, "He's breathing. But he's definitely out." Jacob shifts him into his lap and wraps his arms around Randy, poised for a grappling hold should he wake up.

Dad stares at me, jaw hanging. I lower the clock to the ground, inhaling ragged breaths. As I straighten up I offer him a weak smile.

"*Now* I'll call the police," I say.

He tilts his head back and releases a long breath. His eyes shut, and thick tears spill down his cheeks. I wrap my arms around him again, this time gentler, and burrow in the space between his neck and shoulder.

WARNING (cont.)

If you follow these rules and fail. I will be immensely proud and love you all the more.

According to Jacob, the cop cars, fire truck, and ambulance outside is the most action the cul-de-sac has seen since the last time Mrs. Watkins mistakenly walked into the wrong house. The entire neighborhood stands on the sidewalks, watching as the officers take our statements and paramedics check our wounds. An EMT scolds me for walking on my injured leg, but his condescending tone can't wipe the giant grin off my face. Because in my peripheral vision, Randy is being herded off in handcuffs. And a few feet to my left, an officer is packing the fake will into an evidence baggie. Another cop car is on its way with Andrew in the back seat, headed to us so we can work everything out together, as a family.

Case closed.

Dad is giving his statement with Alanna, huddled side

by side as they recap their experience as captives. And Jacob . . .

My heart sinks when I spot him in the crowd.

Jacob is being yelled at by his parents.

I want to hop off the back of the ambulance and run to his defense. But I've caused Jacob enough trouble by meddling with his family, and I derailed his plan to impress them a thousand times over. So I sit still, but strain my ears to listen (after all, a detective can't *help* but snoop).

"I just don't understand," Mrs. Buckley is saying, brushing tears off her cheeks. "You keep putting yourself in needless danger and it's not *like* you to act out. Your father and I . . . we don't want you around this new friend of yours anymore."

Jacob shakes his head. "Mom, this isn't her fault. I *chose* to do this."

"But why?" Mr. Buckley asks, voice shaking.

Jacob's lower lip quivers. "I didn't mean to scare you. Or . . . disappoint you." He rubs the back of his neck. "I wanted to make you proud. Show you how brave and good I could be, before . . ." He kicks a pebble across the sidewalk, shoulders sunk. "Before my sister comes. In case she was the daughter you wanted all along."

Mr. Buckley blinks. "*That* was why you did all of this?"

"I know I wasn't what you guys expected," he says, wiping a tear from his eye, "but I just . . . wanted to show you I was still worth it, so I didn't get replaced."

Mrs. Buckley places one hand on her stomach and slowly lowers herself so she's kneeling on the sidewalk in front of Jacob. She grips his arms and stares into his eyes.

"You could *never* be replaced," she says, eyes teary but voice firm. "Your father and I *love* you. More than we thought it was possible to love someone. And when your sister comes," she says, rubbing her stomach, "we won't love you any less. We'll just learn to love more, like we did when we had you."

Mr. Buckley places a hand on her shoulder and gives Jacob a serious look. "We're already proud of you, Jacob. We're proud of everything you are."

Mrs. Buckley cups his face in her hands. "You're the bravest person I've ever met. Braver than I could ever be." She smiles warmly. "You don't have to prove that to us. We already *know*."

Jacob's chin quivers and he wraps his arms around her in a tight embrace. Mr. Buckley ruffles his hair. I smile to myself as I watch, feeling like a weight has been lifted.

My dad's voice carries across the lawn. He's still with the officers, and when I glance over, my eyes meet Alanna's. She offers me a soft grin and tilts to the side, bumping her shoulder against Dad's. I can't make out her next words, but she nods toward me and gestures for Dad to go. He smiles gratefully and—in a motion so fast I almost miss it—brushes his hand against her back before heading my way. I have a *lot* to ask him about his time held captive with Alanna and Mrs. Watkins, but all the questions dissipate as he makes his way toward me. I leap off the back of the ambulance and rush toward him, ignoring the EMT's objections.

"Dad!" I swing my arms around his waist and squeeze with all my might. "I did it! I solved the case." I loosen my grip to look up at him. "Are you proud?"

He sighs. My stomach drops.

"Of course I'm proud . . ."

I swallow. ". . . But?"

Dad bends down in front of me. His fingers brush my curls from my cheek. He tucks a loose strand behind my ear. "Remember when I said I loved that you kept your mother's memory alive through solving mysteries?"

I wince. "You take it back?"

"Of course not. I never want you to stop honoring her, or loving her, and keeping her alive however you can. I *love* that about you." He runs his thumb over my cheek. "But I never want you to risk your own life by trying to extend hers. I never want *you* to stop living or *us* to stop living our fullest lives. That's not what she would want either."

I take his hand in mine and run my fingertip over his bare ring finger. Although I can't see it, I know he has our family photo nestled in his wallet. Out of sight, but still there. "That's what you were trying to tell me before you disappeared, right?"

"I'll never stop loving your mom. She was the brightest, kindest woman I've ever met . . . next to you," he adds with a soft grin. "But—"

"I know." I stare at my shoes, doing all I can not to cry. "I used her book at first, but then Andrew stole it, and I solved the mystery anyway. In the end . . . I was able to do it on my own. Without her."

Dad tilts my chin up with his thumb. "That's not a bad thing, Pepper. That's a *good* thing."

"How?" I ask, tears bubbling up. "I started sleuthing to feel closer to her, and now she feels farther away than ever."

"Your mom didn't leave you that book so you'd live by it word for word," he says. "She left it so you'd read it and *add* to it. So it could belong to *both* of you. Be something you made together, even if she wasn't here to finish it with you."

I wipe my eyes. "She said that?"

Dad smiles. "She didn't have to."

He tugs me to his chest and gives me a tight squeeze. I nuzzle against his neck and close my eyes, imagining it's just the three of us here together for one last moment before I say what I have to say next.

"You've been gone for *days*," I start.

He withdraws. "I smell, don't I?"

"Well, that. But I was thinking that you've had a lot of

alone time with Alanna. Minus Mrs. Watkins, that is." A few yards away, Alanna's chatting with an officer. I can't hear much, but suspect he's asking her about Randy. Despite the furrow in her brow and bags beneath her eyes, I catch her glancing Dad's way every few seconds. "With Randy out of the picture, it sounds like she's very, very single."

And I need to apologize to her, too. Eventually. I wanted to believe she was the murderer, so I could keep my family to Dad, my mom, and me. I've held on to Mom so tight, I didn't make room for anyone else. Not the girls at West Higgins, and—in some ways—not even Dad.

But our family is changing. I've made room for Jacob and Andrew. Now I have to make room for someone else— for Dad's sake.

For that loneliness he mentioned all those years back— the one I felt too, but was too scared to name.

Dad's ears turn red. He shifts to the left, as though forcing himself not to look back at Alanna. "Pepper, we're not—"

"I'm a top-notch detective, Dad. The amazing sleuth that solved Great-Aunt Florence's murder. You think I can't put it together when two people are flirting?"

He shakes his head and laughs. "Okay, fine. But two can play that game. How about that boy you're always around, then?" He nods across the sidewalk toward Jacob. "Does your father need to have a talk with somebody?"

My face burns bright red. "It's not *like* that, Dad!"

My cheeks refuse to cool as I realize this is my opportunity to tell him the truth. Somehow this is just as scary as facing off with Aunt Wendy and Randy.

"You can't assume I have a crush on every boy I hang out with," I start.

He chuckles. "I know, I'm sorry—"

"Because sometimes I might have crushes on girls, too."

My face had to be redder than my hair at this point. This could all end up being for nothing; I was still confused and unsure what those feelings about Ashley meant. But Mom said to follow every hunch. And if I was going to become my own detective, that meant including Dad in my cases.

Even the personal ones. *Especially* the personal ones.

"I haven't solved this mystery yet," I say, refusing to look up, "but just in case the clues end up leading to something . . . I thought you should know."

When I look back up, Dad has a gentle smile on his lips. I already feel relieved enough to cry.

He reaches out and I prepare for a comforting embrace. Instead, he scoops me up in his arms. I'm definitely too big to be carried, but I'm not about to complain; it feels great to be off my injured leg. More important, it feels good be held—especially after sharing the truth.

"We have all the time in the world to figure these

things out, sweetie," he says, voice soft against my ear. "That's what I'm here for, remember?"

I nod, biting back tears. I'd held on to Mom's *Detective Rulebook* like it was all I had. Tortured myself with memories of losing my West Higgins friends like there was nothing left.

But then I made an ally in Jacob. And finally—after ridiculous stakes dragged it out—realized Dad had been my partner too, just like he'd been Mom's.

And he always would be.

I tighten my grip around his neck. Dad starts to carry me across the street, back toward our house. Mrs. Watkins turns away from Alanna and the officers and waves her arms toward me.

Dad lowers me back down. Mrs. Watkins hobbles over to me and takes my hands in her cold, veiny ones.

"They told me everything, dearie," she says, eyes shimmering with joyful tears. "Your great-aunt Florence . . . she *saved* me. And so did you."

"You're the woman my aunt left her fortune to," Dad says with an understanding nod. "As soon as we move our things out of the house, it's all yours."

"About that," Mrs. Watkins says, releasing my hands. "Florence's inheritance is going to save me from living in a nursing home and will afford me my own private nurse. So if it's all right with you, I'm going to stay right where I am, in the home my husband and I built."

"With your owls," I say, grinning.

She nods. "With my owls. And as for Florence's house . . . I was hoping to sign it over to you."

She looks up at my dad. He blinks fast and adjusts his broken glasses.

"Mrs. Watkins, we couldn't—"

I yank at his shirt. "Yes, we *can*. And we *will*." I point across the street at the mansion. "Look at it, Dad! It's a *thousand* times better than our apartment in Connecticut. And you and I have unfinished business here." I give his shirt another tug and whisper, "Alanna—"

"Even if we owned the house, we can't move here," he says. "My job is in Connecticut. We'd have no income—"

"You'll find a job," I insist. He rolls his eyes, gearing up for an objection, so I add, "In the meantime, the mansion can be our income. We can make it, like, a museum, and charge entry fees. Andrew and I will give tours and tell the story of the greatest, most terrible murder mystery this town has ever seen."

"Pepper—"

"*Or* we can make it an inn, and rent out all the extra rooms. There are *tons* of ways to make money off it. And we'll be right across the street to keep Mrs. Watkins company," I say, giving her hands a squeeze.

Dad chuckles. "A museum or inn? Are you trying to lure weirdos into our home to create more mysteries to solve?"

My eyes bulge and my grin doubles in size. "You called it our home."

He laughs, shaking his head, then leans down to scoop me back up. "We'll talk about it later."

We head across the street, toward the mansion. Pieces of the dolphin's head float in the fountain, and tire marks mar the path leading to the front door. Mom's *Detective Rulebook* is waiting for me in Andrew's room. Once I get it back, I'll do exactly what Jacob suggested: write my own rules, starting exactly where hers left off. I'm not sure what they'll be yet. But when inspiration strikes, I won't be afraid to put ink on Mom's pages—to carry on her legacy with a fresh, new story of my own.

ACKNOWLEDGMENTS

Rule One of Writing:
Publishing is not a journey completed alone.

I am so grateful for the entire team at Simon & Schuster Books for Young Readers, especially Amanda Ramirez, editor extraordinaire. Thank you for believing in Pepper and Jacob's story. Your sharp editorial eye and unrelenting support not only made this book possible, but also made it stronger than I ever imagined. Thank you, Morgan York and Jen Strada, for your copyediting, and Krista Vossen and Aveline Stokart for the beautiful cover and jacket design.

Thanks to Jennie Kendrick and the team at Red Fox Literary. There are no words to express how grateful I am for your support, dedication, and fierce faith in me and my work. I'm the luckiest writer in the world to have you in my corner.

Thank you to my fellow writers—Nicole Melleby, Seth Hickenbottom, and Julia Nobel—whose feedback and insight helped transform *Pepper* from an idea into a story. And thanks to the mentors who taught me how to write along the way: Donna Freitas, Eliot Schrefer, Coe Booth, Lee Torda, and Rob Sullivan.

Thank you, Mom, Dad, Grandma, and all the family members who have believed in me over the years. Shannon, Hannah, and Vickie: thank you for reading and supporting my stories long before they were any good.

And to Melissa: for hating to read but reading my books, and for loving them almost as much as you love me.